Will You Write To Me?

BOOK ONE

The Courtship of Lizzie Andrews

Published by PJ Watters Books LLC
ISBN 978-0-9908644-0-0

Book design by Nancy Barnes, StoriesToTellBooks.com
Cover design with original watercolor by Michaela Slattery

Image Credits:
Cover image of couple source Victorian Picture Library

Photograph of Lizzie's house on Chestnut Street, courtesy of Robert Buckley

View of Chestnut Street, Salem, MA, source CardCow.com

Day Dresses, *Godey's Lady's Book*, University of Washington Libraries, Special Collections, GT513F37.1800. Fashion Plate Collection

Andrews Children. Oil by C.L. Fenton, painted in 1839. Photographed by Mark Sexton 1975. Courtesy of Phillips Library, Essex Institute, Salem, Massachusetts.

Quaboag Seminary, Warren, Massachusetts, source Warren Public Library, thanks to Sylvia G. Buck

Salem Latin and High School: Oliver Primary School, Salem, Massachusetts, source Library of Congress, Prints and Photographs Division: Historic American Buildings Survey, HABS MASS, 5 Sal,33-1

McLean Asylum circa 1845 from *Frothingham's History of Charlestown*, source Boston Medical Library

Gore Hall, Harvard University Library, source CardCow.com

Dr. Luther Bell portrait by Moses Wight, oil on canvas, 51" x 41" dated 1857. Courtesy of McLean Hospital Archives.

Ladies Rode Side Saddle With Gentleman Escort, reprint of Salem City Directory Advertising Dept. 1859, Permission from Heritage Books, Inc.

Will You Write To Me?

BOOK ONE

The Courtship of Lizzie Andrews

PJ Watters
with Elisabeth Johnson

About the Authors

PJ Watters and Elisabeth C. Johnson

PJ studied writing, theater, filmmaking and dance before earning her B.A. in Art. After writing poetry and a biography of her father, she earned a Master's degree in Health Science and Health Education and worked for two decades as a healthcare executive. Her circuitous professional path led her to become a professional fundraiser. She resides in Spokane, Washington with George Watters, her husband for more than three decades.

Elisabeth earned her B.A. in Art and worked in New York for Carnegie Endowment for International Peace. After marrying A. Albert Johnson and having four daughters, she was widowed at age 35. She moved to California to teach art, later launching a craft business designing stuffed animals and ceramic Pot Pets. An avid genealogist, she researched people in Edward's letters for ten years. She resides with her dog Koko in Washington, Utah and more than sixty gold medals she won for Senior Games archery.

Contents

Acknowledgments

I have to start by thanking my incredible mother for making this book a reality. It took more than a decade of labor to complete the research and writing, but my mother kept us focused and drove the process so the book would be completed by my milestone birthday.

We couldn't have done it without the support and encouragement of friends, families and colleagues. We are extremely grateful for PJ's writer's group at the Spokane Public Library's Argonne Branch for pointing us in the right direction by insisting the story be told from Lizzie's point of view.

Teri Mathis, Mary McCheyne and Barb Willis were our most loyal manuscript readers. Their encouragement, proofing and constructive criticism urged us forward and helped shape this from an epic novel into a romantic trilogy.

Kathy Johnson (no relation) is the best proofreader in the world and we are grateful she volunteered her time and talent.

Special thanks to Nancy Barnes for guiding us through the jungle of self-publishing.

Finally, we want to thank George Watters for his patient, loving support of our efforts over the years.

Foreword

"Hello?" I whispered after the first ring, trying not to wake my husband as I snatched the phone from my nightstand. My mother's voice on the other end was clear, but what she said didn't register.

"You got what? In a dream?" My husband rolled over and covered his head with the quilt as I dragged myself out of bed.

"My great grandmother, Lizzie, came to me in a dream," my mother repeated. "It was so vivid, like she was standing right there at the foot of my bed. I heard her speak as clear as day, 'Tell my story,' she said."

"What story?" The fog was just beginning to lift from my sleepy brain.

"I got all her love letters in the mail yesterday. Sixty-two of them. Letters from her fiancé Edward Tenney. He was only sixteen when he began writing to her. From Harvard. In 1850!"

Now I was awake. She told me my cousin called and asked her if she wanted a box of stuff he found in his father's attic. When the box arrived, she discovered typewritten copies of the letters and couldn't stop reading them. Behind the final letter, she found pictures of Edward and Lizzie.

"Typewritten letters? From the 1800s?" I asked suspiciously, my critical faculties kicking in.

"Lizzie didn't die until 1922. My Grandpa Tommy typed them up," she explained. "The original letters must have been too fragile to preserve. He included a hand-written note about how he tried to figure out the exact nature of their cousinly relationship."

"Cousins? I thought you said they were engaged!"

"They were cousins by marriage!" she interjected. "Grandpa Tommy's note explains. Lizzie's mother and Edward's step-mother were sisters. Grandpa Tommy didn't have access to the internet," she paused, "but I do! So, I'll finish Grandpa Tommy's research and you can write the story!" She said this with the same enthusiasm she often used to announce any number of great adventures she took me on as a child. By comparison, writing a book together sounded so civil!

Before I knew it we were traveling to Boston and Salem to comb through historical society archives, genealogy libraries, city halls and cemeteries.

We began to piece together the puzzle of Lizzie's life, Edward's love and the remarkable times in which they lived.

How *Edward J. Tenney* & *Lizzie Andrews* are related

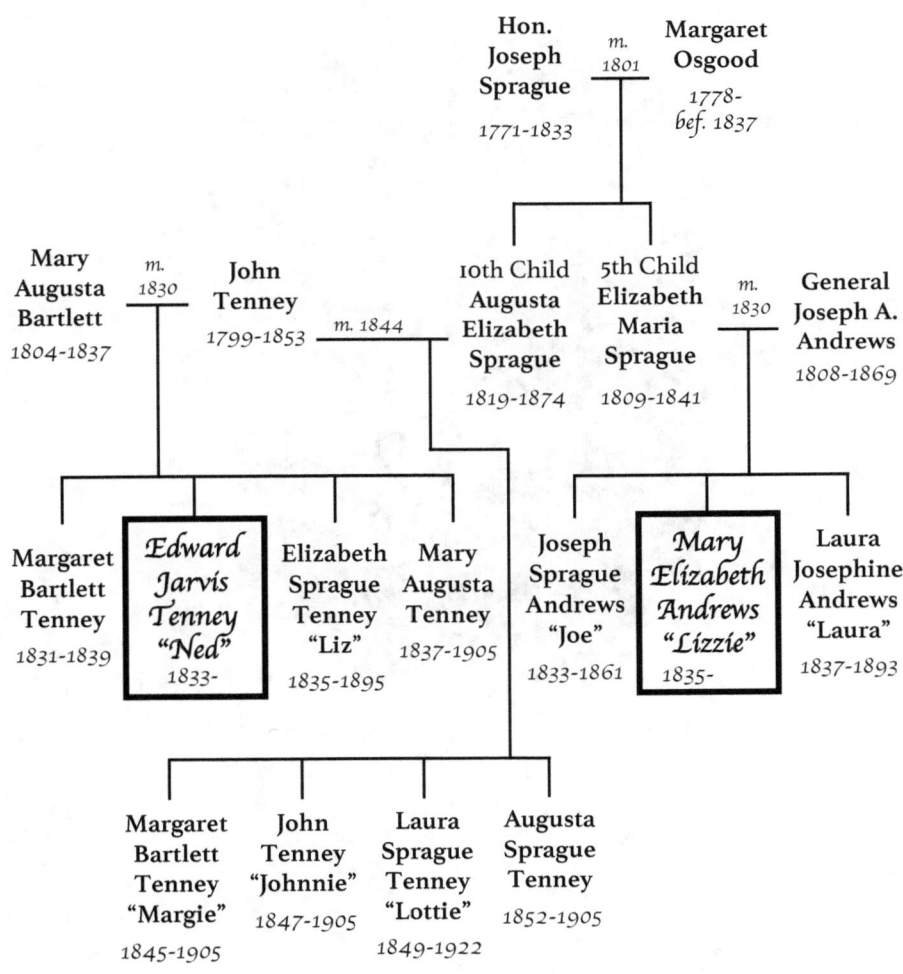

Hon. Joseph Sprague
1771-1833

m. 1801

Margaret Osgood
1778-bef. 1837

Mary Augusta Bartlett
1804-1837

m. 1830

John Tenney
1799-1853

m. 1844

10th Child Augusta Elizabeth Sprague
1819-1874

5th Child Elizabeth Maria Sprague
1809-1841

m. 1830

General Joseph A. Andrews
1808-1869

Margaret Bartlett Tenney
1831-1839

Edward Jarvis Tenney "Ned"
1833-

Elizabeth Sprague Tenney "Liz"
1835-1895

Mary Augusta Tenney
1837-1905

Joseph Sprague Andrews "Joe"
1833-1861

Mary Elizabeth Andrews "Lizzie"
1835-

Laura Josephine Andrews "Laura"
1837-1893

Margaret Bartlett Tenney "Margie"
1845-1905

John Tenney "Johnnie"
1847-1905

Laura Sprague Tenney "Lottie"
1849-1922

Augusta Sprague Tenney
1852-1905

Daguerreotype of Edward Jarvis Tenney 1851

I. Away at Harvard

Edward's letters were written by hand with nib-tipped pens dipped in inkwells. Light came from candles, sun or gas lamps. Relationships were strictly defined and formal. Inscription was slow, formal and deliberate. Communication was courteous and respectful.

His letters have been reproduced in this book as transcribed by Prof. Thomas Oliver.

CHAPTER 1

Ma Chere Cousine?

[1850]
Harvard University,
Sat. Eve.

Ma chere cousine,

Will you write to me? If so, I will proceed; if not, I will end immediately; because, of course you would not wish to receive a letter, which you would not be willing to answer. Therefore, in order that I may do nothing contrary to your desire, I will repeat the query,-"Will you write to me?" As there is no answer, I shall, according to the principle that "Silence gives consent," take it for granted that your answer is in the affirmative, and act accordingly. If I have erred in my premise, I shall consider the not answering of my note an indication of your displeasure and of course must presume that both my letter and myself are highly objectionable to you and will endeavor for the future, to wound your feelings no more. But I can not believe that you entertain quite so bad an opinion of me and therefore will entreat you to write. If but one line, yet do write to me: the oftener the better.

When I bade you good-bye, on my departure from Salem, I felt as sorry and loth to go as it were possible for me to feel under any circumstances. I left the table before I had finished, in order that I might see you once more before you went to school, but I reached the house five minutes too late. You had just gone, and yet as I gazed down Chestnut Street, if perchance I might see and overtake you before you turned at the corner, there was no Lizzie in sight. As I took my seat in the cars, my thoughts again and again carried me to the source of my pleasant visit, and I lamented the summons that called me home, yes home that I wished so much to see. Owing to my long and protracted stay in Salem, I did not go to Dedham and see my sister Liz as I originally intended, but was compelled to defer my visit until some time during the present term.

How do my slippers advance? From a source you little suspect, I learned that they were already begun. Slippers do not need "shoe strings" to tie them, do they?

You may expect me to fly down and spend some Sabbath with you when you little dream of my coming. I shall come down some time with JW. So don't be frightened if I drop down very suddenly some time. But it is 12 o'clock and I have to get up to prayers tomorrow at 5 ½, so I must to bed.

Adieu
Edward
(Do write)

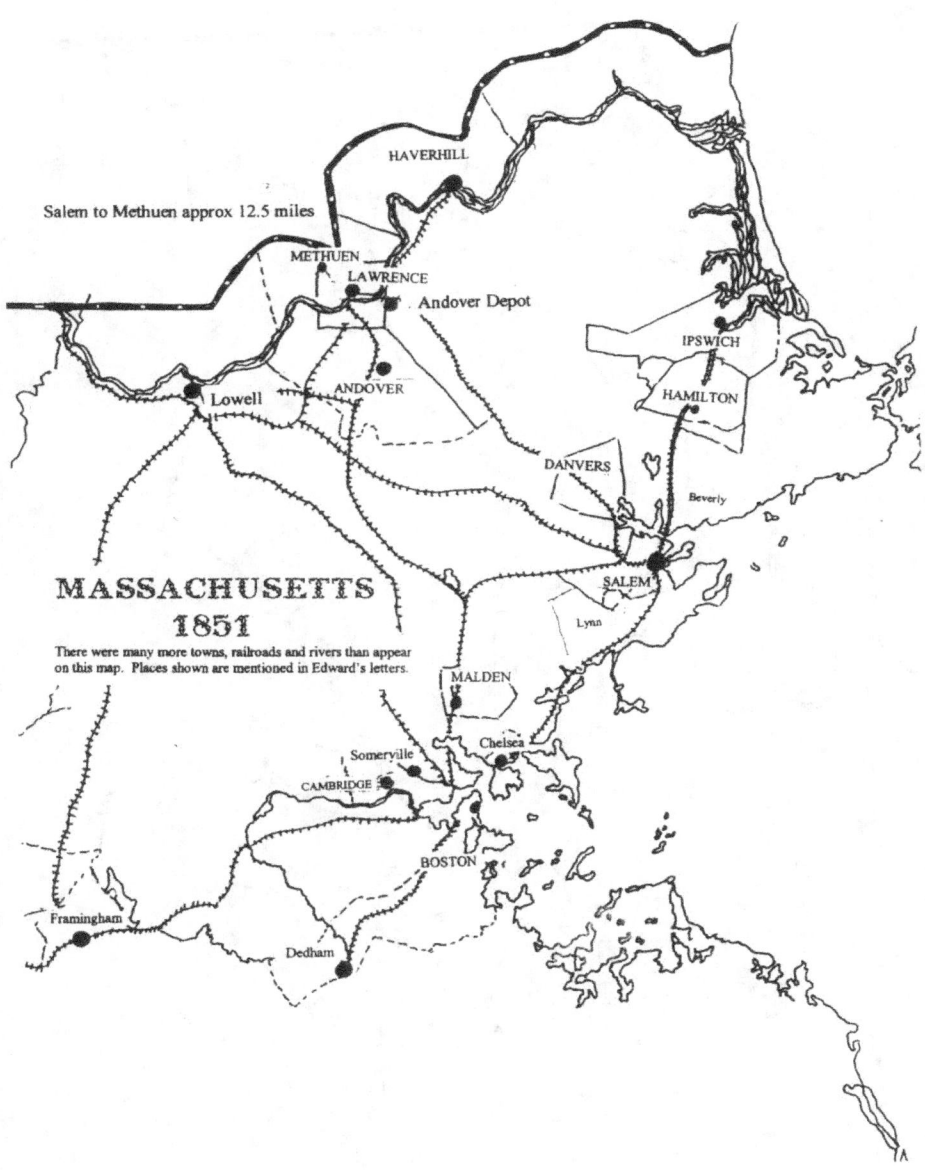

HAVERHILL

Salem to Methuen approx 12.5 miles

METHUEN

LAWRENCE

Andover Depot

IPSWICH

ANDOVER

HAMILTON

Lowell

DANVERS

Beverly

MASSACHUSETTS
1851

There were many more towns, railroads and rivers than appear
on this map. Places shown are mentioned in Edward's letters.

SALEM

Lynn

MALDEN

Chelsea

Somerville

CAMBRIDGE

BOSTON

Framingham

Dedham

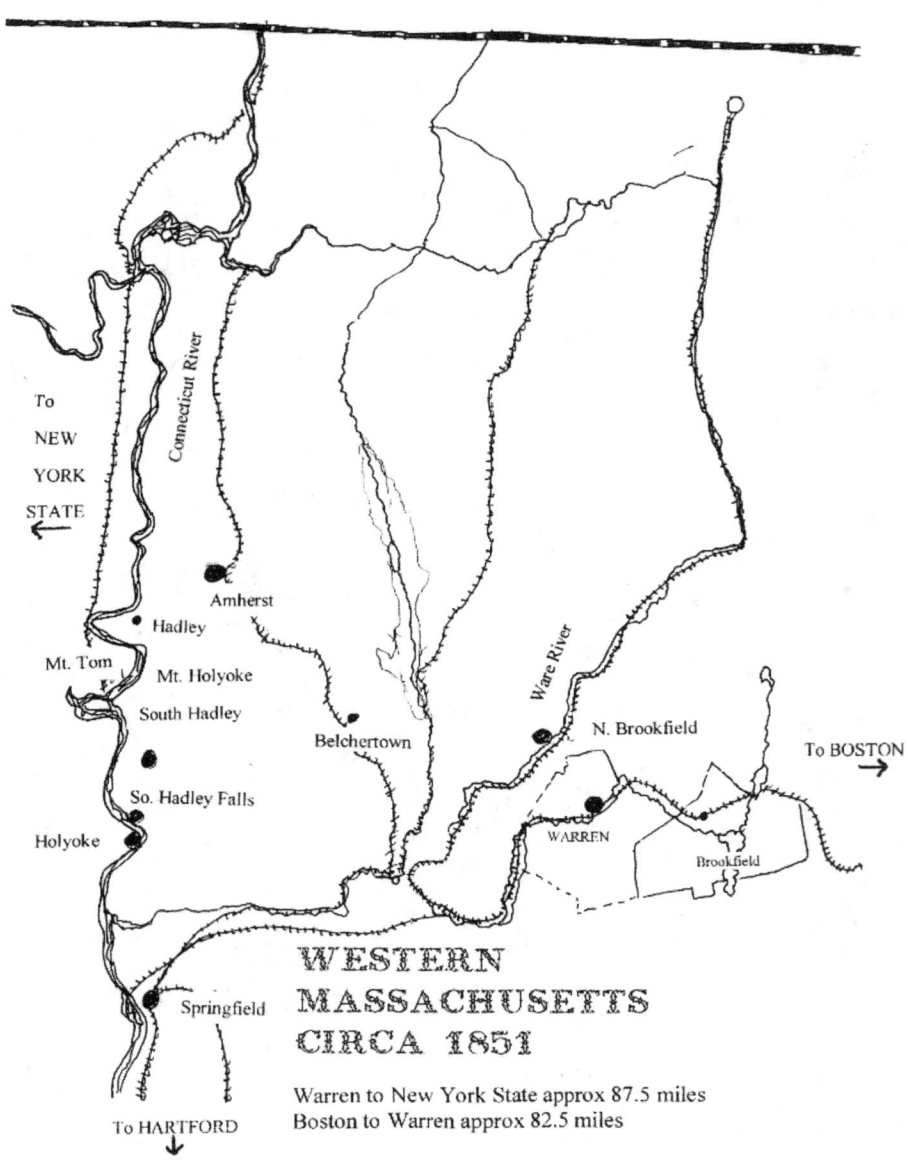

To
NEW
YORK
STATE
←

Connecticut River

Amherst

Hadley

Mt. Tom

Mt. Holyoke

South Hadley

So. Hadley Falls

Holyoke

Belchertown

Ware River

N. Brookfield

To BOSTON →

WARREN

Brookfield

WESTERN
MASSACHUSETTS
CIRCA 1851

Warren to New York State approx 87.5 miles
Boston to Warren approx 82.5 miles

Springfield

To HARTFORD
↓

6

Early 1850

When my cousin was at my home for the recent holyday, I was shocked to see how tall he had grown. So tall and so very charming.

What would my mother say were I to return the favor of a letter to a Harvard scholar? Surely, she would say it is most proper for me to respond to my own cousin. One should not ignore any person's missive! My mother would certainly have advised me—if she were here today. If she were here today, she would provide sweet counsel. If only she were here today.

When she died, I was only six. Edward was just three when his mother departed this earth. That was thirteen years ago! Two years later, his eight-year-old sister Margaret passed on! He says he remembers both burials well. His mother's was during the month of the great harvest in Methuen- one month before his fourth birthday. He recalled many beautiful colorful flowers growing tall from the earth as his dear mother was being planted into a deep hole in the ground. He somehow expected she would emerge the next spring like a flower pushing up from the earth.

I take a deep breath, until my ribs meet the cage of my corset. Lifting my pen, I begin, resolved to respond posthaste to his inquiry... Cambridge must be so lovely in the winter. Perhaps I should not distract you from your studies with a response. Dare you waste your time writing to me? Oh, but you must. I enjoyed your company immeasurably during your most recent visit.

The morning light streaks across my desk, drops to the hardwood floor and climbs my bureau on which sits vanity china from my mother—her water pitcher and bathing bowl—and her ivory-handled, boar bristled hairbrush. I hear the creak of delicate footsteps on the stairs. It must be Aunt Eliza. Dare I request her counsel? She has been everything to me since my mother died. Yet, I hesitate to inquire of her around matters of the heart, as she is my father's sister and might mention as much to Father.

How fortunate we are to have Aunt Eliza, and to her good fortune, we have fine household help. Surely all alone, she could not be our cook and baker, go to the farmer's market and the butcher's. She could not accomplish all that and grow our vegetables and herbs, which I see is her real pleasure in the warm months! How ever would we have survived without her overseeing Margo and Bridget and attending to all the details of our home's needs, not to mention retaining our fine dressmaker? Aunt Eliza keeps a better eye to James than Father can. Why, I have even heard her direct Father's clients to pay delinquent debts with foodstuffs or a cord of wood for winter heat. She sees that everything is in proper order, 'though there is little even she can do about my brother Joe!

My pen tip dry, I immerse it once again to fill, careful not to drop ink where it is not desired. I tell Edward how his slippers advance. He charmed me into fashioning a pair for him. Despite my careful discretion regarding my engagement in such an undertaking, his sister Mary and my sister Laura ventured into my chambers and saw the work was already begun. These girls must be the source of his information about this gift, yet they must not have seen much, or said much to Edward, or he would know that slippers do not need shoe strings to tie them!

I am comforted to know Edward sees JW at Harvard and they have each other's friendship when away from home. Oh, what if he truly were some type of bird who could fly down to spend the Sabbath with me? I close my letter with an invitation for Edward and JW to meet the ladies on Chestnut Street for tea. Perhaps even escort us to a dance at Hamilton Hall. I dare not be so bold as to extend such an invitation to Edward alone. I do not know if he dances before company, but I shall suggest such a soiree might be enjoyable to JW.

And to think Edward hurried his departure so he might bid me farewell again!

Prior to this year, I never left Chestnut Street for my education, having been completely prepared at Miss Ward's school. Hers is one of the best normal schools in Salem.

Studying in Hamilton makes me less concerned for Aunt Eliza, who truly has not a moment's rest with managing Joe's fits and caring for my younger sister Laura as she continues her studies at Miss Ward's.

Lizzie's House on Chestnut Street

16 February 1850

Aunt Eliza must see my excitement when Edward visits, for my heart is leaping from my bodice. She knows just what to do. She diverts Edward's eyes straight away from me.

"Edward, go scoop three cups of flour into this bowl. You'll find the flour barrel in the pantry." He moves so quickly the next word I hear is, "Now, go to the cellar and bring four eggs. Be careful not to crack any."

I keep my gaze on my task, measuring three cups of sugar into another bowl, and then steal a glance as he walks out the back door and disappears out of sight. Aunt Eliza is fixing her look on me. I am intent to keep my joy concealed as I scoop sugar. Edward reappears.

"Now, you may stoke the fire, Edward." Aunt Eliza continues.

I crack and separate the eggs, and begin beating yolk after yolk into the sugar.

"Lizzie, Edward can whip the egg whites, if you like."

"Oh yes, that would be grand." I nod at Edward. "That is the hardest part of preparing this cake," I warn him.

"Edward, they need to be whipped until they are solid white and make a peak when you lift the spoon," Aunt Eliza instructs. He looks at her as if she was speaking a foreign language, but appears to act accordingly, although more and more dramatically as the time passes and his goal is not yet achieved.

"How much time does this task require to achieve the desired result?" he questions, in a manner only a scholar would.

"Would you like me to help?" I ask.

"Goodness, no, I am nearly done, am I not?"

"Yes, nearly," I smile and resist an embarrassing urge to giggle and lean against his frame as he stands at the counter.

Aunt Eliza confirms, "Edward, you can fold your egg whites into Lizzie's bowl, and then help her mix in the flour."

Edward holds his bowl over mine and looks up at me, whispering, "Fold them?"

Aunt Eliza steps in with just a touch of impatience, "Scoop the egg whites into the bowl, a little bit at a time, Edward. Lizzie will show you how to *fold* it."

"Now we mix in the flour, a bit at a time." I continue for Aunt Eliza emulating the seriousness of her tone.

"Can we fold it?" Edward teases.

"Edward, you can scrape butter from the churn for the pan." Aunt Eliza instructs and leaves the kitchen.

Edward and I are alone, and silent. Everything is silent, except my heart. It beats at a frantic pace. I feel his gaze on me and hold my hands as steady as I can to pour batter into the pans, moving swiftly from my post to clean up the mixing bowl.

"There will be sixteen this afternoon at tea," I ramble to break the silence. "Though it is two days late, I think it is never too late to honor St. Valentine," I conclude, remembering how my favorite saint risked his life so others might love.

It was Aunt Eliza's idea to have Edward help me prepare Sponge-Cake for my tea, however absurd it may be to have a man in the kitchen. It is also uncommon for me to be in the kitchen, at least without our Irish help, Margo and Bridget. Those two move so swiftly about to fulfill their duties. Today, they are away to town on errands.

Edward is at a loss in a kitchen, whereas I feel as masterful as a wife. I check to find the cake is rising well in the wood oven and turn back toward him. He is right there, as if he would assist me by pretending to dance with me. He takes my right hand. His is warm. He touches my waist firmly with his other hand! My heart jumps once, and again, as the oak floor board creaks under Aunt Eliza footsteps. She is returning. I jerk my hand from Edward's and turn back to the oven as if I had not just checked the cake a moment hence. I hope he understands my rebuff of his advances.

Aunt Eliza passes through the doorway and Edward declares, "Shall I put this bowl on the top shelf, Lizzie?" as if nothing had changed in the moments she was gone. But it had. Everything had changed for me. I had changed, my practical mind now slipping into romantic dreams.

I wanted nothing more than to linger with my hand in his, his arm reaching around me. I wanted nothing more than to dance with him, at a proper time and place, of course.

"Yes, Edward, that shelf is fine," Aunt Eliza breaks into my dream, and with that she is out the back door leaving Edward and me laughing like silly schoolgirls. I must say I cannot remember when my cousin and I have laughed so boldly.

---

17 February 1850

Though the sun barely lights the sky, I roll myself out of my quilt to meet the winter day head on. Yesterday, after Edward helped prepare the loveliest Valentine's tea, he sadly determined he could not remain in Salem for the party as a storm was expected and he felt he must return posthaste to Cambridge.

This winter has been bitter cold. Most days of late I am chilled to the bone all day and today seems to be no different in that regard. It pains me to dress before the morning fire has time to heat my room. Candlelight lets me ready for my daily travel, for the sun is still straining to light the day.

My petticoats feel as though they would crack from the cold when Father's valet helps me into the carriage. The horse's breath shoots in front of his face like plumes of steam from a locomotive engine. Snow and ice chips fly from behind the carriage as we move forward and the buggy creaks as the wheels turn. Most winter mornings, Father takes me to the train station and sees that I am safely on my way to school in Hamilton before he heads to his office in Boston. Some evenings he does not return to Salem, to avoid a winter's journey. Those nights, I am greeted only by James, our coachman and Father's valet, and of course, our horse Bobby prancing in front of Father's carriage. James talks to Bobby as if he would speak back. Never apologetic, he assures me, "You be free to listen in all yeh like, Miss Lizzie, just doncha let me ruin yeh ears."

James has been with us for several years, since coming from Ireland. He takes good care of Bobby, the carriage and the entire house while Father is away.

A dog barks and a squirrel scampers up the tree. The dog thinks it his job to chase anything that moves down Chestnut Street—squirrels, horses, the lamplighter, the milkman, James and our carriage.

View of Chestnut Street, Salem, MA

CHAPTER 2

———•——✦——•———

Nothing So Difficult
as a Beginning

Edward and Lizzie were born just sixty years after the signing of the Declaration of Independence. The nation was still being formed. Both Edward's and Lizzie's families had a hand in its formation. The cousins were being groomed to take their places in American society.

———•——✦——•———

Miss M. Lizzie Andrews
Salem
Massachusetts

Friday evening April 5th 1850

Dear Lizzie,
    "Nothing so difficult as a beginning
    In poesy, unless perhaps the end." Don Juan, Canto 4.
    Perhaps you will think me very silly for commencing this letter with a quotation, and that a poetical one, but I will incur the

danger of encountering your displeasure, and trust that this will be entirely effaced from your memory before we meet again. At all events, after attempting such a thing, I shall not dare to make my appearance in Salem till I am confident that all remembrance of this letter has gone. However, I would, by no means, have you, for a single moment, entertain the idea that this is any sign of sentimentality on my part. If such a thought should chance to present itself before you, and if you suppose, from the heading of this sheet, that I am growing sentimental, I would call your attention to the past, and beg of you to consider whether, during my recent visit to Salem, I gave you the least reason for judging me guilty of such.

To be sure, one Sunday evening, when you were all reciting extracts of poetry (Psalms, I believe), I began to repeat "Scott's Death of Marmion," which so shocked you, on account of Religious feeling, I suppose, that you were on the point of leaving the room, and I prevailed upon you to remain, only on the condition that I would keep silent and sit at least ten feet from your majesty. That scene put such a damper upon my poetic feeling that I never dared again to make the attempt in your presence; though I afterwards found that you were excessively charmed with my singing Psalms and advised me to join some Operatic Company, which I have well considered and have finally concluded not to waste my vocal powers, with those so far inferior to me, viz. Truffi, Beneventano &c, but to wait till Jenny Lind visits America, and to accompany her, should she offer me a sufficient inducement.

After such a demonstration of your hostility to Poetry, as I saw in Salem, be assured that I should not dare to make the present attempt, were I not at a sufficient distance from you to protect my ears from a severe boxing. I do not mean to say that you would box my ears, but such a thing has happened to my knowledge and may possibly happen again. But enough! Two pages are already filled with nonsense of the very worst kind and it is full time to say something. And what shall I say? I know not what will most interest you and suffice to fill this sheet.

I have not yet been to see Sister Liz, which it was my intention to do as soon as I found an opportunity. I should have gone two Sabbaths ago, had it not been for Mr. Nichols illness. Liz has left Aunt Margaret's and is now either at her teacher's, Mrs. Capen's, or in a large white building, which you have probably seen, upon the bank of the winding Spicket in Methuen. Mother wrote to me that if possible, she would board at Mr. Capen's for the present, and if he was unable to accommodate her, she would return home instanter. I wrote to her last Saturday and shall do so again next Sunday. I intend to pass the coming Sabbath in Malden at Lucy Barrett's, but shall return during the evening and write to Liz before morn.

Let not your expectations of my visit to Salem soar too high, to receive the greater blow when they fall. For I have been conversing with mine honored pater upon the subject and he seems to think I have already tarried there too long and that it would not be prudent for me to return again so soon. As a dutiful son, I shall of course regard my father's advice as a command and forbear for the present. Perhaps before this term closes I may make you a short call. Nothing would certainly afford me greater pleasure; but perhaps you are tired of me, having staid three whole weeks at your house, doing no one any good except making Sponge-Cake and frequently troubling you. Meanwhile you and I will converse as well by mail, as if there was nothing to separate us, and we will not permit distance to prevent or oppose our intercourse.

I have taken two lessons in dancing, and have not yet made much headway; I am not yet able to dance with you "the Polka, cotillion or Redowa," (I do not know what that last is, perhaps a fisherman's Hornpipe). I have unfortunately entered near the close of a quarter and can therefore receive but few lessons until next winter, if I chance to attend again. Our class is not very large, four only, and there are none but males. Mr. Papanti's regular class consists of about twenty boys and he has another class of girls, who are taught separate and not as in Salem. I can imagine what "splendid times" you have dancing and only wish that I could join you.

Words can not describe the pleasure, the heartfelt joy that filled me upon the reception of your letter. When I penned my short note to you, at the beginning of the term, I hardly expected, ardently as I desired, an answer, fearing that you might be afraid to write to your green and simple country cousin, of whom you seemed shy when he was in Salem, and then I might not receive a reply for years. But now that you have expressed your willingness to write occasionally, you know not what pleasure it will afford me to communicate to you my humble thoughts. The happiest hours of the whole term will be those I spend in your company through the medium of pen and paper. Writing no longer seems a task and if the whole day were as the few moments I steal this evening, Earth would be to me a Paradise, and in my thoughts dull care, Greek or Latin would ne'er find room and Trigonometry the worst of all would obtain but little sympathy from me.

Oh had I - (I was going to say "the wings of a dove") a pair of seven-league boots not a sun would set before I had followed this letter and held oral conversation with ma chere cousine. But 'tis late, and I must write to Joe before morn; therefore I am compelled to close abruptly and let me entreat you to write when you find time.

Good night! Good night! Good night!
Ever your affectionate cousin,
Edward J. Tenney

12 April 1850

Jenny Lind is coming to Boston! I do not imagine I could partake in such entertainment as he does with great frequency.

Still, Jenny Lind is the great talk of the town. Never have I seen so much excitement for any singer! Oh, that I might hear the magic of her voice. It is purported to be so much larger than one might expect from someone of her slight stature. We are told she must be heard and seen by one's own person to be believed.

This week I have re-read Scott's Marmion. I would like to know how it came to be so imbedded in Edward's memory that it would burst forth with such disruption at our gathering. I do admit, although shocked with the timing of the recitation, I was secretly charmed.

Edward does not seem to recall Psalms from memory, yet he spouts forth with a most irrelevant poetry that he has carried back from Harvard as this.

> "Alas! That Scottish maid should sing
> the combat where her lover fell!
> The Scottish bard should wake the string
> the triumph of our foes to tell!"

> O, Woman! in our hours of ease,
> Uncertain, coy, and hard to please,
> And variable as the shade
> By the light quivering aspen made;
> When pain and anguish wring the brow,
> A ministering angel thou!—

His courage and boldness do disarm me for when he demands attention, it is difficult to look away from even a most outrageous performance. He approached me outright as he bellowed the phrase "coy and hard to please" and ended with a courteous bow to me as if beckoning for an angel to minister thou.

Oh, mercy me, the way my cousin fires up a room, turning my nature from its gentle course to one of recklessness just short of a motherly ear-boxing. I must remain composed for fear too much relaxation in his presence might expose how he affects my disposition.

Edward's deep voice seems much larger than he is, as well. Why, his voice fills the parlor and the library and I am certain it could rattle the dishes in the dining room cupboards when he bellows along with the piano.

Edward portrays himself as a country boy when in fact he is an accomplished scholar at one of the finest schools we have.

---

19 April 1850

Today is my fifteenth birthday. Since it is Friday, I will take an early train from Hamilton and prepare to celebrate with my family this evening. Grandmother is coming for tea at 4:30 and will stay for supper. By the time I return home, I expect to smell my favorite foods; roasted chicken and fresh-baked bread. For dessert, cake, of course, and a toast to me with a cheering round of speeches to guide me through the next year.

---

2 June 1850

The Ancient and Honorable Artillery Company celebrates its 212th anniversary tomorrow under Father's command. They have beautiful new uniforms. Laura and I saw Father's and she told him he looked extra tall in it. He says Aunt Eliza will take us to Faneuil Hall in Boston where a formal dinner is to be held and he is to give a speech. We are to be the only children present, but as we are his special guests, he is confident we will behave as the poised young ladies we are becoming, and Aunt Eliza is to assure we do.

Perhaps the military waits until the best season, with the longest days, to march, to train and also to wage battles. June seems to be the most active month for military ceremonies, or perhaps all ceremonies! The 75th Anniversary of the Battle of Bunker Hill is on the seventeenth in Charlestown. I expect we will participate in a ceremony there also, as Father is in command. He said the Governor, Honorable Edward Everett, is the Orator and many thousands are expected to attend. Class-day at Harvard occurs on the twenty-second of this month. For me, the occasions make a grand topic for letters to Edward, lest I see him there in person, in which case a letter describing my joy in visiting with him would make an even grander topic for written discourse.

Edward has visited again! Although too brief, we had a lovely ride and I do look forward to his company. After each visit, I can hardly wait for the next!

Street map of Salem, Massachusetts 1851, showing residences

1. General Joseph Andrews
   38 Chestnut Street
   Lived with children and his
   sister Eliza

2. Andrews Family
   24 Lynde Street
   Grandmother Andrews lived
   with her children Daniel
   Andrews and Dolly Ann
   Watkins

3. Dr. William Stearns
   384 Essex Street
   Built by Dr. William Stearns
   Land later bought by Gen.
   Joseph Andrews

4. Grandmother Sprague
   Corner of Essex and Dean
   Streets
   Occupied by Dr. William
   Stearns and Sarah White
   Sprague family; then by
   Joseph E. (Stearns) Sprague

5. George and Priscilla Sprague
   92 Federal Street; Adjoined
   by home of Rev. Octavius
   Frothingham family

6. Gen. Henry K. Oliver
   142 Federal Street
   Built by Captain Samuel
   Cook

7. Malvina T. Ward
   home and school
   34 Chestnut Street

8. Rev. James Thompson
   40 Chestnut Street

9. Saltonstall Family homes
   39 and 43 Chestnut Street

10. John C. Lee
    14 Chestnut Street

11. Dr. Abiel Pierson
    Barton Square

12. Post Office

13. Salem Latin and High School

14. Hamilton Hall

I gladly remain inside this blustery Saturday morning thinking what to write to my cousin Edward that will not seem shy or too personal. I fetch a biscuit, thankful it is baking day and sit for a moment to warm my insides with hot tea before settling in to write. I plan to finish my letter in one day and take it myself to the Post Office. I do not want Father to see it, as I will not have him anticipating the reply! However, I am certain when Edward responds Father will take notice for he carefully observed the arrival of my last letter from Edward. As he handed me the posted letter, he raised one eyebrow. That was all. No questions were asked. Yet.

Certainly I could adequately answer any of Father's inquiries should he wish to hear about my correspondence with my cousin! Will he think it curious that Edward never wrote us when he studied at the Bird's? Or last year when he was at Phillips Andover Academy? Or that now he is posting his letters specifically to me? I would tell him Edward and I have found comfort in writing about our mothers. Truly, we have talked about the strange coincidence of both grieving so young and missing our mothers.

I put pen to paper: Edward, you must include some news of your studies on occasion so the next time Father asks I may impress him with something learned of the classics.

If Father persists, knowing I have received more than one sheet of paper, I may also tell him Edward and I write of the coincidence that neither his father nor my own took a new wife for quite some time. That will give Father cause for silence.

Edward's father remarried seven years after his mother's passing. Father has not remarried, though nearly a full decade has passed since Mother died! I could simply ask Father, "Do you know any widowers who have not remarried in a year or two, besides Senator Tenney and yourself?" I do not. Most young widowers remarry or send their children to live with relatives. Perhaps that would not be best to say lest he think I was asking to be sent away. Well, then again, perhaps he would send me to live with my cousin Liz Tenney!

Oh how boldly I can speak to myself when I know I would never reveal a bit of this insubordination lurking within me. If the truth be told, any inquiry from Father would result in my cordial reply and an unrelenting exposure of every incident that ever occurred with my cousin not that there is anything to speak of! We broke bread together and sang at the piano – perhaps out of Father's sight but always in the presence of others.

CHAPTER 3

———— ⚬⚬⚬ ————

Prompt and Eager

Most of the people Edward mentions in his letters enjoyed the privileges and prosperity resulting from a good education, as well as from their old New England families.

———— ⚬⚬⚬ ————

Miss M. E. Andrews
Care of Col. Joseph Andrews
Salem
Mass.

Cambridge, [Thursday] June 20th 1850

My dear cousin,

You see that I keep my promise with great, perhaps you will say, *too* great fidelity and that I am very prompt and eager to answer your last letter. Yet do not think that my haste arises from a desire to perform my contract and have it "off my hands." By no means is such the case, but ere three days have elapsed since I saw you, I find myself impelled by some indescribable, irresistible power towards this delightful recreation, which, though it may cost me a tutor's displeasure, should I be called upon to recite, is well worth even that price. I have a holyday tomorrow and another on Saturday yet something may occur at that time to prevent my writing and I dare not trust the future. Moreover, I have several letters to write during that period and I choose that one first which will afford me the greatest pleasure.

I have not yet written to Liz to make your request but shall do so on Saturday next. Perhaps she will not have the courage to commence a correspondence, but I will use all my influence to induce her to comply. The only *sure* way to have an epistolary intercourse with Liz is to write the first letter yourself and then she will answer it and afterward derive a great deal of pleasure from writing as well as receiving. I wish that you would say to Liz when next you meet that I told you she did not write to me often enough. It may have a good effect and induce her to write, at least, one letter to my three. Do not, however, tell her that I requested you to say this but let it seem perfectly voluntarily on your part. I received a letter from her today of *almost one page in length* and she made that answer for my last four letters. Perhaps you may think I am doing very wrong thus to discourse about my sister, but I tell it to you in order that you may repeat it and a much greater effect will be produced than if it came directly from me.

Tomorrow is class day and we have no duties to perform, except to attend morning prayers at six o'clock. In the afternoon there will be a collection and dancing in "Harvard Hall." None but the graduating class have anything to do with the direction of it, although they (the Seniors) have the privilege of inviting friends to join. I have received a request to participate in the enjoyments of the day, but declined the honor, inasmuch as I hardly feel well enough acquainted with dancing to trust a display of my accomplishments "before company."

I hope, notwithstanding Aunt Laur's fears to the contrary, that the horse reached Salem in safety on Monday evening after our very short drive. That was the first ride I had had for some time, and though it was not of very long continuance, I enjoyed myself very much indeed. Perhaps I can say it was the pleasantest ride I had ever taken. But I promise myself more such during your visit to Methuen.

There are only three weeks to look forward and then I shall have six weeks of unrestrained relaxation. I have almost abandoned my intention of requesting permission to spend a portion of my holydays in Hartford and I am inclined to believe that I shall derive more pleasure by remaining in Massachusetts. I am certain that a portion of it, at least, will be passed more agreeably than if away from home.

I think that I acted very foolishly on Monday last in permitting you to return to Boston before you had seen the procession. Had I known where they were to pass, we could easily have seen all and I suppose that I could even have obtained admittance for you in the Hall and you could have heard the Oration if I had known at the time that such a thing was possible. But you appeared to be so very much troubled and so anxious lest you should keep me from the procession &c that I hardly knew what I was about and thought the only safe way for you to be free from the crowd would be to return to Boston. I think however, that you did not lose very much by your departure, because the house was so crowded that it was very difficult to hear the Orator even for those who sat near the stage.

I have not yet requested leave to spend the coming fourth of July with you though I am very much inclined to believe that I shall meet with a refusal, since Father fears very much that all such things draw me from my studies.

Saturday morning [June 22] -- You must excuse this breakage in my letter, for I was summoned to recitation on Thursday when I had written thus much, and during Friday I was kept busy the whole time. "Class day" is the day for receiving friends and classmates and I should have found it utterly impossible to have written two lines without interruption except between the hours of 12 and 2 and then I myself was absent from my room. The Oration and Poem of the Senior class were delivered at that time and nearly all of the students were present, besides a great number of ladies from Boston, Cambridge and all the neighboring places. After these exercises there was a short dance on the green and then all adjourned to Harvard Hall where dancing was continued till after six o'clock. At this time the Seniors, having marched around the yard with the band at their head and cheering every building as they passed, danced round the "Liberty tree," singing "Auld lang syne" and in a few moments the war-cry of "Harvard" was raised, when the other classes rushed in and danced with the Seniors at a furious rate, not, however, after Mr. Papanti's rules; yet only a few in each class were seriously hurt. My room-mate was knocked prostrate but did not receive any serious injury. Many others had their heads and noses broken, though none were killed. In the evening, the Seniors attended the lever at Edward Everett's and the members of the other classes went off in different directions, most of them to return very late some sober and others intoxicated according to the usual custom. You must not think that I was one of the latter. Far from it: I remained in my room nearly the whole of the evening to "entertain company."

Do write to me soon, and with my regards to all, consider me ever

Your affectionate cousin
Edward

P.S. Since the above was written I have seen Father. He says that I may go to Salem the 4th of July or go during the vacation, just as I choose. I would prefer the latter since I can stay longer. I am very sorry, but there is no help. Good bye

———— ⟨∞⟩ ————

30 June 1850

Edward judges himself foolish for permitting me to depart Charlestown before the Bunker Hill procession was complete, yet I initiated taking my leave to avoid the jostling and raucous behavior of so many pressed together seeking entry to where Edward Everett was speaking. Never before had I seen such a rambunctious crowd. Why, I am surprised people in this crowd were not hurt as they were at Harvard during the class-day celebration! It was shocking how well-bred persons clamored like sheep to be admitted to hear Governor Everett speak. I do not think they would have been able to see the governor in any event—see him, perhaps, but hear him, not ever! Not over the din of such an eager crowd. His oration at the Bunker Hill celebration drew 10,000 persons, albeit larger in numbers than the crowd at Harvard, the former gathering was likely more civilized than the latter!

Mr. Everett can speak understandably to any group it seems, which marks his acclaim more than his tenure as professor of Greek Literature at Harvard and subsequent advancement to president of that very college. Today, Jared Sparks presides over Harvard, yet Mr. Everett graciously returns to give orations, by popular demand, I am sure. Although I do not regret leaving the bedlam, I am sorry I was not able to hear Governor Everett's speech that day.

After my abrupt departure, I hope little time passes before I see Edward next, as I do not want the memory of how we last parted to linger in our thoughts. He will not come to Salem until late summer. Before I begin my studies, however, I expect to visit Methuen in August, for I have been invited by Aunt Augusta and Aunt Margaret to spend several days at the Tenney residence. I am sure to enjoy time with Liz, if she is not too hurried in her departure for Dedham. I do wish she would write to me so I know her wishes.

6 July 1850

The festivities to celebrate our country's independence from British rule were met with a most pleasant sun-filled day. All the community, women and children included, gathered outside filling in every city park and village square to see the Liberty Pole raised after which school children of all sizes paraded their colors to the cheer of admiring crowds. Picnics were everywhere with games of marbles and town ball with spectators turning cream and ice to enjoy as a treat in the afternoon sun. Groups of musicians play wherever people gather. Speaking platforms spring up on most street corners for men are eager to pay tribute to our nation's founding fathers. And not only men!

I heard a lady speaking publicly on a platform by the train station where Father, Laura and I stood. She spoke eloquently of her grandfather who lived in Boston seventy-four years earlier and had witnessed the Boston massacre as a young boy. Never before had I heard a lady provide any type of Oration. She drew quite a crowd—some hissing at first, but after a while all fell quiet and attentive. She bellowed a charge to the crowd, particularly to the men, to think about the meaning of the constitution, and remember how ladies are the mothers, wives and daughters of every man who fell on the battlefield risking their lives for our freedom from taxation and foreign rule. She cries: Each of you has sprung from the loins of a woman. Each soldier among you has been nursed back to health after battle by no less than a woman. And while you were at battle, who is left behind to carry on? Women, she answers herself, gesturing with a fist toward the sky. She does not stop there, but continues: Despite loss and grief, women carry on for they have children to bear and rear. She chided the audience to give praise to the women who feed and clothe men, who serve the tea that is at the center of tea parties great and small. I begin to feel very nervous for her making such a fuss, thinking she must be eager to complete her story, but she seems comfortable winding her tales with all eyes upon her. I watch Father listen with utmost respect and, as I turn back to the speaker, I feel his eyes turn to me. He seems to be observing my intent as I watched this most outrageous, yet impressively bold, lady.

Women today have become more assertive, perhaps out of necessity. Many have lost fathers or husbands at sea. Why, Lucy Barrett even signed for the transfer of her family's property on the corner of Essex and Beckford, which Father purchased at auction last year. Imagine that for a woman! Lucy received it from her grandfather, Dr. Stearns, and had no need to retain property since she is now married to Henry Barrett. I cannot imagine what Father has in mind for this property.

---

1 August 1850

Father has been appointed a Justice of the Peace for the County of Essex. Aunt Eliza says it is a position for which he is particularly well suited as he has had much experience keeping the peace in this household! She must be thinking of Joe, for her comment certainly made *me* think of Joe.

Fashions for September 1850.

Day dresses from Godey's Lady's Book

21 August 1850

Edward rode by horse from his home in Methuen to Hamilton Friday last, just for the day. We had the most glorious weather as if it were the peak of summer, rather than near the end. We walked for several hours in the afternoon and, I dare say, I saw places in Hamilton I had never taken notice of before. The scents of the late summer were more glorious than I ever remembered.

"There are trails just outside the town that allow one to peek through the trees and across a small valley to view the nature high on the hills," I told Edward as we strolled, my arm laced through his. The leaves are beginning to change color—not brilliant orange and yellow, but a few are scarlet and several deep gold birches emerge from the foliage as a striking contrast. There are fading wild flowers on the hillside that I have never noticed before, for I have not before been quite this far from the boardwalks of Hamilton's main street.

As Edward turns to lead us back to town my dress brushes against the rough bark of a tree. The tree was so near the trail it actually caught my skirt and a thread of green beads popped off from one of my silk bows. The beads scatter wildly on the ground bouncing like little bugs in every direction. I cannot easily retrieve them, for my corset is laced rather snugly. Edward drops to his knees searching for the tiny things. Alas, only a few are visible.

"I feel I have caused such a bother, I do not know how to thank you for your trouble," I confess.

"Let me keep one bead to remember our day," he suggests.

"Of course," I am pleased to oblige. I dare to ask, "But, what will you do with one green bead?"

He rolls the bead between two fingers and holds it up to the sun. Closing one eye, he looks at it and says, "In the sun, it is nearly the color of your eyes." He looks at me and continues, "Stunning. On your dress here, it reflects the warmth and beauty of your eyes." He begins pointing to the beads remaining on my dress. Imagine that, such a sentimental sort—like I have never known.

He places the bead in his watch pocket and says, "I will find a place near my heart for it." He puts his face very close to mine as he speaks and I can feel his breath on my cheek. I can see my own heart jumping against the bodice of my dress; I fear he can see the same. I look into his eyes, a deep blue, the color of the sea, so clear that I can see the reflection of the sun on my hair in his eyes.

He says no more, and then gazes at me with such a look as I have never seen. I do not utter a word for I fear I will swoon, but kept my composure and suddenly blurt, "I think you are very … cunning indeed … though your eyes are *blue*." I dare say I turned crimson hearing myself speak in such a manner to my cousin, and I began to laugh out loud with such nervousness that I laughed until I could barely draw a full breath. Edward was compelled to join me as we concluded truly the nicest walk I have ever had.

---

1 September 1850

I have been making arrangements in Hamilton, before the weather turns, to board with one of my teachers during the week. Alas, I will not interrupt my studies with daily travel in the railroad passenger cars, but return home at week's end. So, I am gathering my belongings to prepare for such a stay. I shall pay one final visit to Methuen before settling in Hamilton for the fall and winter seasons.

Father brought me a trunk so I could pack my belongings for Hamilton and I found it was not empty. Inside was a carved wooden box. Father looked at it and then at me saying, "You may look through this, if you wish, Lizzie. This box pertains to your Mother." He did not leave me alone, but sat at my bedside and watched as I carefully lifted the box lid. I found a printed notice about my mother from the newspaper from nearly ten years prior. Father sat still and silent as I read it aloud.

Salem Gazette dated Friday, September 3, 1841.
Mrs. Elizabeth M. Andrews

We copy from the Christian Register the following beautiful tribute to the memory of a lady, whose life was one steady current of cheerfulness and benevolence, who never saw a wound she did not endeavor to heal, a sorrow she did not attempt to soothe, or a want that she did not relieve. She was indeed the mother of the orphan, the stay of the widow, the heroic and devoted wife. And of her devotion to the duties and charities of life, her own premature death is no doubt the result.

For a journey in the sickly season of the last year, to the State of Missouri, to take to her bosom the beautiful orphan of a deceased sister, has terminated her earthly career.

We said her death was premature; but we were wrong. A life rich with so many virtues is always ripe for the harvest. An ornament for the religion she professed, we trust she now reaps its fruits in a region —Reg.

I looked at Father. He said not a word and made no attempt to leave my side. He nodded as if to say, "Read on." So I did. The article continued with a quote:

> "Where persecution enters not,
> Where sorrow is unknown,
> And tears are never shed."
> In Framingham, 4th inst.

I paused and, as if Father could hear my thought, he said, "Yes, it was the fourth day of August that your mother died; exactly nine years ago today." He looked over my shoulder and read "at the residence of Dr. E. A. Holyoke."

"Please continue," he pleaded.

I read,

"Mrs. Elizabeth Maria, wife of Joseph Andrews, Esq. of Salem, and eldest daughter of the late Joseph Sprague, Esq., age 31.

The announcement of this death struck us, not with surprise – for it was expected; not with grief, though she was a friend; but with a certain feeling of unreality, we do not know what other word to express it. The subject of it was one of those who seems NOT "born to die," whom we cannot associate with the images which the thought of death calls up. The narrow coffin and the damp, dark grave, seemed not made for her. The thought of her was mingled with the things of life, with the circle of friends, with kind words and offices of sympathy, with glad spirits, with the fresh air and bright skies.

And it is ever the case that we find it difficult to associate the idea of death, with those who, …"

Father recited the rest of the sentence without looking at the page, "…in the fullness of life, are yet peculiarly prepared to die."

Although two pages remained to be read, I fell silent momentarily and Father waited ever-patiently for me to speak.

"It is a beautiful tribute," I said. "I feel I did not know my mother. I did not know Mother died at Dr. Holyoke's!"

I did not know a thing of the tragic situation about Lucretia, so Father spoke to me of my mother's sister, Lucretia.

"Your Aunt Lucretia was three years your mother's junior," Father explains. "She had been weakened from childbirth, but was fighting to live. Your mother had been worried about her sister ever since baby Lucretia was born."

Father expected consumption took the new mother's life. After Aunt Lucretia died, Mother was going to bring the baby daughter to live with our family in Salem to be raised as a sister to me and Laura.

Father's voice cracked when he told me, "Their brother, your Uncle Edward Sprague—born just a year before your mother—also died of consumption. Only one year after your mother passed."

"What a tragedy for their whole family, for our whole family!" I lamented, "I could not bear the feeling of my own sister dying!"

Even now, nearly a decade later, Father seemed very sad to talk of my mother's death. As he continued his story, his eyes glistened with tears but not one drop fell.

"You are old enough to appreciate this tribute," he cleared his throat and pointed to the pages that remained in my hands. "With each loss your heart breaks, but it breaks open, and the family's love grows stronger." I felt a heaviness in my chest, and a great fondness for my strong and gentle father.

"We are born to make the world a better place for those who live now and those yet to be born. That is plainly the purpose and the duty of our lives." I did not reply but simply stared at the newspaper tribute, trying to control my breathing from becoming too rapid.

"I miss your mother terribly and think of her every day, but I know she is at peace with God." Those were his parting words to me, but I had more questions, so rose to follow as he began to ease his way out of the room.

"What happened to baby Lucretia?"

"The family took care of her."

"Who? Who took care of her, Father?"

"One minute, Lizzie. I want to show you something more." He led me to his study and retrieved a page. He handed it to me and I read to myself.

Joseph G. Sprague, Salem, Essex, MA. Wife Priscilla, our daughter Carolina Augusta, adopted daughter Lucretia Thompson shall be supported, educated and instructed as our own child; that they may ever share in each other's love and affection, as sisters of the same family and bound to promote each other's welfare here and to pursue together and encourage each other in the path to Heaven where through sovereign grace may we all again meet.
Signed 27 Mar 1844, Joseph G. Sprague.

Witnesses: Henry Cook, James C. Briggs, Joseph H. Town.
[Probate file 416-488 Essex County]

"When was she born, Father?"

He pondered, "1839 – She was two years old when her mother died."

"Then she is nearer Laura's age than mine." We sat in silence.

"Do you remember meeting Lucretia?" he inquired. "You were just six years old when your mother brought Lucretia home. Joseph George Sprague came to our home to welcome her to his family. Perhaps you remember meeting Mr. Sprague for after speaking with him, you told me you thought he was a very kind man."

"I do recall a particularly quiet snowy day, one of those days when the snow makes everything seem very bright, and he drove up in a grand carriage." Father nodded, as if we were looking at the same picture.

"You ran to the parlor window when you heard the horses outside and pressed your face against the glass. The moment he entered the house, you ran to him and asked if he would go get your mother in his carriage."

"I do not remember asking that."

"He had the same dark eyes and hair as your mother and looked as if he could have been her brother, although he is her cousin."

"Our family's own history fits closely with our country's history," Father continued. Father often used family stories as a way to teach history to me and Joe, so I settled myself in a chair prepared for a lesson.

"Your mother's grandfather, Joseph Sprague, lived in Salem and was a Major of the Massachusetts Militia. He fought in the war that freed us from British rule."

Father pointed to the painting on the wall above the fainting couch. "Your grandmother Margaret Sprague gave you the doll you are holding in this painting. You were five years old."

"I still have the doll, but do not remember Grandmother Sprague. I hardly recall my own mother."

Andrews Children. Oil painting by C.L. Fenton, circa 1839.

We stared at the painting as if we had never seen it before. How absurd that I had passed it daily for years and not really thought much about it. After a moment with no response from Father, I said, "Aunt Eliza seems like my mother. I am *very* glad to have her in my life," I exclaimed, feeling grateful, with perhaps too much enthusiasm.

Father chuckled and said, "So am I. So am I." With that, the lesson concluded with an encouraging word to me, "You will know your mother better if you finish reading these tributes about her. I will leave you to do so. I expect Aunt Eliza will check on you soon to begin your packing for Hamilton. He left the room and I got to know my dear mother.

"They adorn life, and it seems that death should spare them. They are sweet flowers, planted in life's borders, and it seems that their beautiful heads should not be bowed in the dust. They seem peculiarly made to live, to be happy and to make others happy, and we cannot bring home to us the thought that they have gone down to darkness and silence. Nor need we think thus. They have not died even from the earth. Only their names have left us. Their memory is fresh in many hearts that keep beating on with life's hopes and fears. All that was best of them lives in its influences; as flowers spring up when the turf has grown green over their bodies. Above all, decay has no power to touch that we lived in them. They still live. They have indeed left our circle—but it was to join a brighter one. The farewell that they have spoken to us is changed for a welcome from lips that have no touch of mortality. They have left behind only the troubles by which they were surrounded, and life, real life, has begun to them—a life for which this world is but the birthplace and cradle.

She, whose departure we are noticing, was one to call up such thoughts as these. But it is no part of our purpose to enlarge upon the character of one who was little known out of the circle of her immediate friends. That circle was, indeed, large, but it needs not to be reminded of her excellencies and virtues. All, who knew her well, will bear witness that her life embodied much of Christian spirit. It was adorned with those peculiar graces which the religion of Jesus calls forth from a woman's heart."

A tear dropped from my eye to the page and I tried to blot it up quickly with my handkerchief. But that only served to open the floodgates for more tears poured forth, with stuttered breath, and I could not contain myself. I let down the page completely and tended to an upwelling of grief and sorrow that came from I knew not where, yet I was helpless to do anything but let it surface. It took me several moments to compose myself for I wished to finish this tender visit with the mother I knew far too briefly. The mother who had been buried in a forgotten part of my heart. The mother with no notion how she touched others. The mother who, through the same gentleness she gave so freely to others, loved her own children.

The tribute drew a sweet conclusion:

"Gentleness in her was sweetly mingled with a determination that shrunk from no duty—tender sensibility with a sustaining fortitude. The lovely traits of her character were the regard of those who knew her, as her virtues had secured their esteem.

Beautiful as were the ministrations of her life, her death was yet more touchingly beautiful, called from the midst of life's duties and enjoyments, with much to live for, and surrounded by those who looked to her for counsel and sympathy, she heard the call without a fear or a murmur. She seemed to have no will of her own. The Divine will was her will. She gave herself up to it with the most childlike trust, and at last fell asleep in it calmly as an infant child in its mother's folding arms.

Of such a life only happy remembrances are to be cherished. For such a death no tears of bitterness are to be shed."

———❦———

8 September 1850

I am in Hamilton now after my visit to Methuen having arrived Friday last, only to find Edward had already departed to Cambridge. Disappointment aside, I had a very enjoyable visit with the girls and the children, who were quite active and excited for my company! I do hope to see them all again before too long. They greeted me upon my arrival with the enthusiasm often reserved for visiting dignitaries.

"Libbee! It's Libbie!" Little Johnny yelled as he ran to meet me at the gate. Mary had prepared afternoon tea for the little ones outside on a picnic blanket in the grass.

"Look, Margie. It's Libbie. We're habbing a pih-nik, Libbie!" Johnny said, as Mary grabbed my hand and pulled me toward the blanket.

"Johnny, her name is not Libbie," Margie said with the sweet sternness of an older sister. "Say Liz-zee."

"Lib-bee," Johnny repeated the same but more slowly.

"Libbie," echoed Lottie in a babbling murmur.

Little Johnny becomes a shadow to anyone who can read as he trails behind, his primer in hand, asking, "What is this word?" Sweet Maggie seeks constant assistance in any number of senseless projects that bring a smile to her face as she bangs pots and pans one minute and builds a castle of them the next. Baby Lottie is happy and content as can be to fall asleep in anyone's arms. I dare say I miss them all myself! The cheers they emit when one pays them some mind still ring like joyful music in my ears.

I greeted each child by name with hugs and kisses and gathered baby Lottie into my arms. I could smell her sweet milky breath and feel her warm wet kiss as she turned her little mouth to my cheek. Liz and Mary stood to greet me.

"Oh, Lizzie, I am so happy to see you," Liz said. "I have been day and night with these darling little creatures and I fear I have forgotten how to speak like a lady. Forgive me if I slip and call you "Libbie" myself!" She embraced my shoulders in the most affectionate manner and kissed my cheeks.

"Aunt Augusta is inside," Mary informed me.

"Granpa Eddie is not here," Johnny said.

"Pa Eddie," Lottie made a popping noise with the P.

"Johnny, he's not our grandpa. He's our brother!" Margie gently corrected.

"Yes," Liz said, "You just missed Edward. He will be so disappointed."

"I know the feeling," I shared, and filled Liz in on the arrangement I had made to stay in Hamilton. Mary continued her work on a beautiful needlepoint and Margie poured pretend tea, not caring that the tea pot had already been emptied.

We were content for some time to sit outside. One minute Johnny would run around, bat at leaves with a stick and collect an occasional spider or grasshoppers. The next minute he demanded attention with his primer. Such energy!

Finally, Margie enticed us to gather wild flowers to bring inside for the supper table. Liz said she was surprised any remained since this had been a regular activity all summer for Margie.

Mary stayed with Lottie, who seemed as happy as a baby could be and we followed the other little ones through the grasses and around the trees until each had two fists full of rapidly wilting flowers. By the time we came around, the picnic had been cleared and Mary and Lottie were inside helping Aunt Augusta. Uncle John seemed cheerful but subdued and he excused himself to prepare for dinner.

The evenings were spent reading, mostly passages from the Bible, which was a common activity, dare I say entertainment, in which the children could show their reading skills and practice their oration.

The week went quickly and I returned home for the Sabbath and, once again, proceeded to gather my things for Hamilton. Departing my home in Salem Monday morning for Hamilton spurred much anticipation, feeling as though I was truly no longer a child, as I embarked on an entirely new routine.

CHAPTER 4

⸺ ❦ ⸺

Grandpa Eddie

In the 1800s, teenagers expected to forgo their own personal desires to fulfil their family obligations. Such duties were necessary to support their families. Edward and Lizzie were fortunate to have the luxury to pursue their dreams for their futures.

⸺ ❦ ⸺

Miss M. Lizzie Andrews,
Care of Col. J. Andrews,
Salem
Massachusetts

Cambridge, [Wednesday] September 25th 1850

Dear Lizzie,

I am very sorry that I was not able to pass the last week of my vacation with you at Methuen as I expected before I left Hamilton But on reaching home, I ascertained, to my great dissatisfaction, that our term began much sooner than I had anticipated and back to Cambridge I must go, notwithstanding the plans I had made for your visit. No sooner had I arrived here than I learned from Mother that you were in Methuen and I found that I had left home two days sooner than was really necessary. That was comforting to me truly, but there was no help and the utmost that I could do was to wish you a happy and agreeable visit.

I think you must have found plenty of flowers, and I hope that you had a pleasant time although the girls were obliged to attend to their duties at school during the whole of your short stay, I think. But there was Johnny and Margie to amuse you, and even Lottie must have aided somewhat unless she happened to be in a mood for crying the whole time, which would be something very strange. I think that Lottie is growing quite cunning, although she has blue eyes, and it pleases me very much to hear her say "Grandpa Eddie," which she now does very readily.

I returned home on Saturday last to pass the Sabbath and as soon as I entered the house, I took her in my arms expecting of course that she would not recognize me but would begin to cry. The cunning thing however, clasped her little arms around my neck so prettily and rested her head upon my shoulder so lovingly that I was almost enraptured and felt like carrying her with me to Cambridge. And throughout the day she would not allow herself to be taken from me but was continually playing around me and repeating "Eddie," "Eddie," "Grandpa." But for all that Johnny is the chick of all chicks, in my opinion and he often tells me about his going to Col. Andrews and seeing "Libbie."

I had some faint hopes of meeting you at our house last week, as Liz had not informed me, in any of her letters, of your departure although I thought your school was to commence before this. I wish you could have staid longer, because you come to Methuen so seldom and then only for a few days that one hardly has an opportunity of seeing you before you are gone. You are expected to make us a good long visit during your next vacation and you must not disappoint us on any conditions whatsoever.

I received a letter from Daniel Upton of Salem today, urging me to come to Dr. Holyoke's this evening where I would meet "my cousins and all the Chestnut Street ladies," that is Rose Lee, Mary Thompson, Margie Phillips &c &c I suppose, but as I had heard nothing before about going to Salem I was very much surprised and was at a loss to account for the meaning of his letter. But I came to the conclusion that there was to be a grand party and that he, supposing I had received an invitation, was kind enough to send me his assurance that I should have a fine time and to request me to come if possible. But even were that the case I could not have neglected my college duties for so long a time since I have but just obtained leave to pass two days at home and another would not now be granted, unless in case of a marriage or death. If there was a large party and you enjoyed yourself as I hope you did I shall expect some account of it from you.

Two members of our class have been just dismissed from college for harassing and disturbing the peace and quiet of divers Freshmen who seem to find their rooms rather uncomfortable for themselves some times and who are subject to have pails of water thrown on them from the upper windows, *accidentally*, of course. It is very foolish, I think, for Sophomores to expose themselves to the danger of expulsion merely for the sake of sprinkling a poor Fresh, but there are some nevertheless, who will go on in spite of warnings and injunctions from their tutors and the faculty. Every one in the class pities the fate of the unfortunate victims but nearly all are compelled to pronounce the sentence just.

Jenny Lind has at last reached Boston and soon a few select will have the pleasure of listening to her "sweet, entrancing voice." I hope that you can induce your Father to consent that you may attend one of her concerts before she leaves New

England, and if you succeed I wish you would send me word when you shall come, and perhaps I will also go at the same time, since I desire very much to have the pleasure of saying that I have heard the Swedish Nightingale and the gratification of accompanying you would be fully sufficient to induce me to make an attempt to obtain a seat among so many competitors. But if you do not succeed in your request, I think that I must, for the present at least, forego the pleasure of hearing Mlle. Jenny, since my love of music alone is hardly enough to induce me to pay $5.00 or $10.00 for one evenings entertainment. I have already heard several songstresses whom my poor knowledge of music would probably pronounce as good as Jenny Lind, but still the reputation of the latter is my greatest motive in desiring to hear her. The announcement of the first sale of tickets is very surprising and it is nearly thrice that in New York, $625 being paid for the first seat, or rather for the reputation of having paid that price for a single ticket. I do hope that you can hear her before she leaves Boston. Everything is "Jenny Lind" now; there are Jenny Lind beds, Jenny Lind boots, cigars &c. &c.

Every time I open my "porte monaie," I am reminded of a certain afternoon's adventures in Hamilton, by the appearance of a small green bead, which never fails to meet my eye, and which perhaps you have not forgotten. Almost every day I think of that whenever I see this talisman and it is really amusing that I can not forget it unless by the removal of its cause.

But I must bring to a close this long letter, which though tiresome to you is still very pleasant for me, and turn my attention to the barbarous Greek. Tell Joe that I am expecting a letter from him every day and that I should be still more happy to see him "in propria persona" at Cambridge. I know that you will write and so good-bye for the present –

Ever yours
Edward –

Jenny Lind has arrived in Boston! Edward told me his great uncle, Dr. Jarvis, proposed the introduction of theatrical entertainments to the legislature forty years before Edward was born. Dr. Jarvis convinced the legislature that a play—if it is selected well—would instruct the mind, improve the morals and elevate the sentiments of the spectators.

According to Dr. Jarvis, 'Youth would be diverted from low pleasures and demoralizing amusements by such recreation.' I have no trouble imagining such boldness in the lineage that led to Edward!

I have been forewarned many such entertainments are indelicate, so I would not seek attendance without very good reason—although Edward's persistence would be reason enough for me! I do not understand why some, such as Dr. Jarvis' own friend Samuel Adams, would attempt to prevent theater from coming to Boston. These two were chums who otherwise agreed on nearly all issues but this! Mr. Adams felt theater could more likely cause people to misbehave. Edward has been witness to an audience protesting a performance at the opera when the singer suffered from a cold, though I cannot imagine people really behave so. I trust Edward would not say such if it were not in truth more offensive than even he describes.

When Father handed me Edward's letter he seemed to linger until I sat down and opened it. I desired to savor it in the privacy of my room, but did not want to give him reason to think this was anything more than an innocent letter from a cousin. So, I sat in the parlor and read my letter while Father read the paper. When he asked, 'How is Edward?' I was perfectly prepared to give him a response. Father seemed satisfied and asked no more, turning his attention back to his pipe and paper.

For me, however, what Edward wrote about those Harvard fellows was truly shocking. Shame on them for how they treat the new scholars! It is completely barbaric. The men who caused so much trouble for the

51

poor freshman should rightfully be expelled. It causes me great concern for Edward's safety and I should hope he removes his person from the presence of such unkind behavior. Of course, he would not indulge in such ribaldry himself, but it poses a challenge to remain clear of these troubles—especially for someone like Edward whose disposition compels him to embrace all social gatherings. Fortunately, he is likely to be one of the few remaining attentive to maintaining order among those who imbibe in excessive spirits.

———————⟨❧⟩———————

28 September 1850

Dr. Holyoke hosted a grand affair last evening. I wish Edward could have accepted Daniel Upton's invitation to attend. Edward's father escorted Aunt Margaret and Aunt Augusta. Nearly forty persons were present, including many of our cousins, the Chestnut Street ladies—Rose Lee, two of her sisters, Mary Thompson and Margie Phillips, who arrived with me on a train from Hamilton. Liz came from Dedham. So it is plain, had he been able to attend, Edward would not have been the only one to travel some distance to this soiree.

Rose Lee's father inquired of Senator Tenney as to Edward's whereabouts, saying he is "glad to hear Edward is taking his Harvard studies seriously." I moved closer to the parlor to partake of this conversation, as Mr. Lee announced to a guest his status as a graduate of "Harvard - class of 1823." I know not why Harvard graduates note their class year, as if it were a particular credential. Margie Phillips' mother and brother, John, were there. Her father, the Rev. Phillips, engaged Mr. Lee to compare stories of Harvard. I staid just long enough in the smoky parlor to hear Mr. Lee say he returned to Harvard for a Masters degree some years ago. I wondered if he had known Representative Edward Everett personally before he became Governor of Massachusetts.

Throughout the house, conversations were lively. I heard the Honorable Leverett Saltonstall mention the new Fugitive Slave Act. Saltonstall was the first mayor of Salem, as far back as 1836, which would have been when I was just a year old. He was known to be a most reliable source of information on the law. Of course, Father says he provides it from the perspective of a Whig.

After casually overhearing conversations among the men pertaining to items of much greater interest than those of the girls my age, I would bring the news to the girls. I was pleased to be allowed to linger among the men. I plan to tell Edward who among the gentlemen present were from his honored college. I wish him to think me clever for recalling every detail of this very distinguished group.

Dr. Holyoke said, by way of introduction, he and Father seemed to have much to discuss of a serious nature regarding banking, commerce and investments et cetera—matters I simply could not endure for long. It was a grand and lively affair, though I preferred to join the ladies by the fireside.

Among my peers, Leverett Saltonstall seemed to be engaged in quite a pleasant conversation with Rose Lee. I know not the specific subjects of their attention, therefore, Edward will know nothing of this either! Why, they were so utterly engaged they nearly missed most of the party's festivities.

I conversed with Margie Phillips and she commented "Edward is one of the finest sorts I know." I shall not tell Edward this, however; for it could give him too much pride. Besides, I suspect she has a special fondness for my cousin and it is certainly not my place or my best interest to tell him such. He is the only gentleman she ever mentions. Margie displays great modesty around men. Not so with her lady friends. She can be quite daring as when she suggested the two of us ride alone in the cars to see Jenny Lind in Boston. Neither of us dared to ask our fathers to pay $5.00 for such an amusement at the great risk our fathers' displeasure, not to mention the risk of social scandal should we be seen as two young women on such a venture.

At the mention of Jenny Lind from the men in the smoking parlor, Margie clutched my arm and nearly dragged me to the men's parlor to hear what more was being said. At first I thought Rev. Phillips spoke of a gentleman suitor of Jenny Lind's, but as we got closer I got an earful.

"Phineas Barnum has arranged for Jenny Lind to make diverse appearances, at quite commanding ticket prices," Mr. Lee remarked.

Rev. Phillips responded, "She has only been in this country two or three weeks and already has received quite favorable acclaim."

"Yes, it is said she provided a splendid performance at her debut on September 11 at the Castle Garden Theater in New York, the first of nearly a hundred performances scheduled for her in the States. She is taking quite an extended stay from Sweden," Mr. Lee commented, as Father joined the conversation.

Rev. Phillips responded, "She commenced her European tour in London singing for the Queen, who praised her voice."

Rev. Phillips added, "Did you know that Verdi wrote that role of Amalia in the opera *I Masnadieri* specifically for her?"

Rev. Thompson had been listening in, and interjected, "Though she no longer performs opera on account of her religious convictions. She has made this news quite public." Both Mr. Lee and Rev. Phillips looked askance.

Rev. Thompson explained, "I am not assured that her arrangements with her manager and promoter, Mr. Barnum, are entirely appropriate." Mr. Lee's expression went to one of shock and disapproval.

Now Father shocked me with his knowledge by saying, "Initially, Mr. Barnum paid her $1,000 for each concert and paid all her expenses, yet still was able to keep a great deal of profit for his own trouble so, once she arrived in New York, the payment arrangement changed and he agreed to give her fifty percent of the net profits, which only seems reasonable. Well, she earned more than $12,000 for her first performance!"

"It is quite unclear if he is a business manager or a suitor! Certainly he does not behave with the benevolence of a father, but rather seems to have some other designs," the Reverends nodded knowingly to each other.

Mr. Lee remarked, "The cost of a ticket is as much as a doctor charges for a night house call."

Rev. Thompson offered, suspiciously, "Jenny Lind received twice as much for her first performance as I paid for my home, remarkable for a lady, and for one of only 29 years!"

Father, eager to compare economies, seemed to ponder Reverend Thompson's remark. I could not detect whether he mused over Jenny Lind's youth or the value of Rev. Thompson's home—the latter more likely occupying his attention. For me, however, knowing that Jenny Lind was so old intrigued me!

---

4 October 1850

Father is at his annual military encampment for two days with the 6th Light Infantry. Hundreds of troops gather from all over the state. According to Father, encampment duty is required by law to assure the infantry is fit and orderly should they be called to duty. Joe says Father simply likes to go camping.

I delay my return to Hamilton a few days to be present at some of the festivities surrounding the annual affair. So many men in uniform change the color of the landscape from green and brown to blue and gray, save for the occasional spot of color from a lady observer. I recognize Emily Oliver, a dab of red taffeta among the guests, and join her with her father. I am absorbed into their world as she watches her brother, Samuel, accept an award for the unit he organized in Lawrence and now commands. I watch him as well. Oh, absurd! I cannot take my eyes from him. His lanky height gives him a truly striking presence. Taller than Edward. My own father presents his award. I think he nearly measures up to my father in height! Emily thinks I am watching my father, but it is Samuel who has caught my eye; yet it is Edward who has caught my heart.

---

23 November 1850

I have not heard from Edward for quite some time and, just today, Aunt Laur tells me he has left Harvard! Surely she teases me to say this, for I can scarcely believe he would do such a thing! I beg her to confess her announcement is merely for her own amusement, but she insists it is true! Now, I cannot doubt she tells the truth, but she cannot explain the situation. Edward would not leave of his own will. He could not be failing in performance of his scholarly duties. What else could it be? "He has been dismissed by the college…" Aunt Laur says "…for violating college rules."

Now, I *do* have reason to give his ears a good boxing, but truly I am concerned. Harvard is his dream. How can he follow the lead of his own father as an esquire without the education necessary to pursue such a profession? Oh, I am dismayed. He must be full of despair. Why I, myself, am filled with despair. What is to become of him? Why would he not write me to give me this news in his own words? I will correspond promptly and confess what I have heard and implore him to explain.

CHAPTER 5

Disgrace and Dismissal

There was no question Edward needed a good education to prepare him to take his proper place as a social, business, religious or political leader in society. In the 1850s, a Harvard education was thought to be the best. A girl of Lizzie's social standing was also expected to be well educated. Finishing schools, available to girls at the time, prepared girls to be teachers, a highly valued vocation for unmarried women. Schooling was an important vehicle for socialization and for instilling the moral values considered essential to America's social order.

Miss M. Lizzie Andrews
Care of Col. Joseph Andrews,
Salem – Mass -
Warren, Massachusetts

[Friday] December 20 - 1850

My dear Lizzie,

Want of courage alone has prevented my writing to you during the past two months, and though, after my disgrace and dismissal from college, I earnestly desired that you should receive some communication from myself, something which might perhaps explain, not conceal the cause of my just punishment, which you did not know, yet I dared not send you any message. Reason to fear I had none, but still there was the thought that it was insulting to expect you to have any intercourse with one who, disregardful of his friends and his own self, had exposed himself to the disgrace of a dismissal from Harvard college. Upon my return to Methuen I determined to write to you, but after destroying sheet upon sheet in ineffectual attempts to succeed I had well nigh given up in despair, when Father told me I could pursue my collegiate course if I chose and then I resolved to write to you as soon as I reached my destination even were it but one line.

Perhaps an account of the circumstances which led to my punishment may not be improper at the present time although it must be painful for you to peruse and for me to again bring forward; because I have learned from Aunt Laur that you knew only of my disgrace but not of the reasons. In this matter I blame no one but myself, and deem that the penalty I have paid for my misdemeanor was if anything too light.

In Harvard college it is contrary to rule to be connected with any secret society, but that law is often disregarded, and I myself, together with many classmates, have been a member of one ever since my entrance at Cambridge. That society held an annual meeting one evening and at the close of the customary exercises adjourned to the "Brattle House" to partake of an entertainment prepared for them by the Freshmen under the supervision of my own class, and together with past members formed a party of about fifty. When we left the hotel almost every one being excited with what they had drank, a great noise of shoutings &c. was made in the public street and the Police interfered to preserve order; one was arrested and then several of his friends rushed forward to rescue him, myself among the number; a policeman captured me, and to free myself I was compelled to give my name, which he found in the college catalogue and then let me go. The next week that officer reported me to the President, who sent for me and demanded the names of the members of that society, and said that if I refused to give them I would be liable to bear the whole blame myself. I instantly refused to comply with any requisition which would bring punishment upon my classmates and the next day was informed that I was dismissed from college until the beginning of my Junior year (August 1851) together with two others who were expelled forever. I think that my punishment was perfectly just and I sincerely hope that it may prove for my benefit and that in future I may evince more strength of character than the past would show I possessed. At first I had not the least idea of ever returning, but President Sparks conversed with me for a long time and advised me to come back again by all means at the expiration of my sentence and rejoin my class as if nothing had happened. He did not blame me for refusing to expose my classmates, but thought in that I acted honorably although the laws of the college compelled him to insist upon that point. When he called me before him to state the vote of the Faculty he detained me in his office more than half an hour talking to me as a son, and as I was leaving, he came towards me and placing my hand between both of his, pressed it for some time appearing really sorry to have me go, and his manner affected me so much that I found it impossible to refrain from tears.

Immediately he wrote to Father, who came to Cambridge and after a long conversation with the president decided that I should return again in August. In the meantime I have to pursue the same studies with my class and for that purpose Father informed me last week that I could choose between Warren and Derry, N.H. I preferred the former and reached this delightful little village at a late hour last evening, and though this is a very unpleasant season of the year, I think I shall be very well situated and perfectly contented during my short stay. I board with Mr. Kimball the principal of the "Quaboag Seminary" a very pleasant man and an excellent instructor and am within a moments walk of Caddie Sprague's, who has a much pleasanter place than I imagined was possible.

Liz intends to make you a visit at Christmas I believe and desires you to teach her to work slippers as prettily as those you were kind enough to make for me.

Do write to me, Lizzie, as soon as convenient or I shall fear that you no longer deign to correspond with me since my disgrace, which perhaps I deserve from you as another punishment for my misconduct at Cambridge and for my neglect in writing to you. Please do not tell any one the contents of this sheet and it would be very gratifying for me to know of its entire destruction, since I have communicated to you what I can to no one else. Don't fail to send to me unless you wish me to consider that my letters are disagreeable; and tell me if you can forget the past, or at least judge me not wholly depraved.

Ever your affectionate cousin
Edward

---

27 December 1850

Oh, Joy! And dread…at the same time. Joy for the letter and dread for the news. What manner of confusion surrounds me as I receive a most meaningful Christmas gift in the form of a letter from Edward. His candid disclosures are shocking but do not hinder my growing fondness for my cousin, which is beyond what I could feel for any other cousin and grows stronger day by day! My letter tucked under my writing desk, I proceed downstairs to see Father gazing momentarily out his study window.

"Father, may I interrupt you?" I ask hesitatingly.

"Certainly, Lizzie. Come sit with me. What troubles you?"

"What is a secret society?"

Father laughs at me, but I do not know why he finds me so amusing.

"It is a secret, Lizzie. That is why it is called a secret society."

"Oh." I was clearly disappointed in his response.

"Perhaps you can tell me why you ask so I might fashion a more satisfactory response," Father still seemed mildly amused, so I tell him what Edward had revealed to me.

"Secret fraternal organizations are not allowed at Harvard. Still, they have been there since its beginning, and will likely endure. These societies, or fraternities, are a source of honor to their members and friendships among members continue well after scholars depart Harvard." Father explains how the members often help each other in business and personal matters for years to come. This explains Edward's loyalty, and the reasons for the defiance he exhibited toward the college rules. I do not fault him. Rather, I think him courageous and brave to protect the whole society and not think only of himself.

I hope his knowing of my joy in hearing this directly from him will bring him some amount of comfort at New Year's. However, I must not encourage his defiance. Secret and special societies are appearing everywhere. Margie's mother even participates in a special society, a temperance society, though it is no secret. Margie has told me men in secret societies are known to carry on for hours and hours with celebrations, completely taking over a public house, often until many a man cannot even stand to walk home. Perhaps it is this behavior that prompts Harvard to keep the not-so-temperant societies a secret. Margie tells me men spend much time, and often much money, in these indulgences. She has been allowed to hear the talk at temperance society meetings in their home. All this will remain secret with me as I strive to refrain from any manner of gossip. Liz Tenney is to arrive tomorrow for several days visit. I do hope she invites talk of the topic!

13 January 1851

Liz has visited for four days, departing in time to reach Methuen for the New Year's Celebration. While she was here, we worked our knitting needles every day – except Sunday, of course, the Sabbath being filled with activities at the First Church in Salem.

Joe attended that day, as he does during the holyday, but not often otherwise. So, the Andrews pew was rather full, as we have little room for guests when we are all five present. Liz, Laura, Aunt Eliza and I all in our fullest skirts, leaves little room for Father and Joe.

"Why must you use so much yardage in your skirts?" Joe grumbled like an old bear to draw attention. "It must be enough for a dozen men's shirts." Father found the situation amusing perhaps because the more yardage a skirt has, the more he is likely to sell, this being the very source of our family's livelihood, which includes Joe!

Then began Octavius Frothingham's sermon, which we found invigorating, but hardly enjoyable, dare I admit. Rather than lifting my spirit with the goodness of our Lord, the sermon challenged us all to imagine ourselves living the lives of those less fortunate, of one whose father or husband or brother was captured and removed from their lives; one whose mother or sister or daughter was met with a fate much worse than he could describe from the pulpit.

Well, these things do not happen in our society, I protested; silently to myself, of course. Not in our time, I insisted. But he continued, and I had to listen as he railed, 'Every day, families are torn apart and we do not protest. We condone this savagery through our own indifference. Why? Why?' The church fell silent. Was he going to answer his question? Then he boomed, 'Because the outside of the man is dark in color! His blood is as red. His heart, as full of love for his family...'

As the service ended and we filed out of the church and shook hands with Mr. Frothingham and emerged to greet the day in which servants, both dark and light-skinned, tended to carriages, waiting to drive parishioners home. Father fetched our carriage as he likes to do on Sundays. Aunt Eliza remained just inside as Liz and I lingered in the Church courtyard, being dusted with snow. Joe remained sour for some time, grumbling about our dresses being the reason not all men are free and mumbling, "excess, such excess." Liz and I paid him no mind and proceeded to engage in lively conversation, only to be interrupted.

"Liz, did you know Mr. Frothingham is 28 years of age?" Joe asks our cousin.

"I did not," Liz responds politely, though her expression reveals she does not understand the reason for the question.

"Do you think him handsome?" he continues to inquire of her.

"Joe!" I reprimand, and enter the conversation. "He is our clergyman, and a married man. That is no way to talk."

Unfazed by my outrage, he adds, "And a relative of ours."

Father drove up and we three younger ladies filled the back seats with our too-full skirts. Aunt Eliza climbed up, with very little assistance, though it was offered, to sit between my father and brother. Conversation shifts to the content of Mr. Frothingham's sermon. Father wants to make sure we value the lesson in humility and are sufficiently awed by the notion that if we look hard enough, we can find more commonalities than differences among peoples, people of every social class, culture and skin color.

By the time Liz left, there was not a scrap of worsted wool in the entire house. We have made New Year's gifts—slippers or mufflers for all the servants in both of our fathers' households. Much to my delight, Liz talked about Edward every day telling me he considers his dismissal from Harvard to be the worst circumstance of his life since their mother died when they were young children. Although difficult to watch Edward endure this, she feels it had a favorable and humbling affect on him, though she says he kept to himself for a dreadfully long time and was filled with too great remorse. I have included Edward in my daily prayers and trust he will have a good outcome to his challenges.

A very nice break from my studies has commenced and I am glad to stay inside a warm house when icy winds blow outside. The ground is covered with a thick depth of powdery snow. Lamplighters trudge down streets seeking paths horses before them plowed open. Nearly every evening since Liz departed has been eagerly occupied reading for pleasure by the hearth. This is not a luxury I often indulge, but the fire flames well into the evening, attracting most of the family to gather 'round, so there is plenty of light for reading. Of course, with all the activity, I often lay my book aside. Father is in grand spirits and never short of a story, or an open ear for company. Grandmother Andrews, Aunt Dolly and Uncle Daniel join us for dinner nearly all twelve days of Christmas.

The grandest feast, of course, is on Christmas Eve. A large turkey roasts in the oven all morning and the array of sweets make my mouth water—persimmon pudding, custard, mincemeat and blueberry pies. Every day is baking day of late with fresh bread and rolls to accompany a roasted ham with cloves and fresh orange slices. Father obtained a large shipment of fruits, so we enjoy a cornucopia of fresh, sweet oranges and exotic mango and papaya fruit I have never seen before.

Bridget and Margo work in the kitchen for days on end. They seem to have a fine time with the preparations. Laughter draws me to the kitchen where I spot James hanging mistletoe to dry with the sage and rosemary above the kitchen sink. Each time Margo goes to pump water Bridget declares, "Here comes James!" Margo shrieks and jumps away, splashing water out of the sink and all about her in a frenzied effort to avoid his advances. I cannot see James; however! He is nowhere to be found! Bridget teases Margo the whole of the time; though Margo may know the prank, she still does not resist the thrill, or the fear, maybe the hope, she might be caught under the mistletoe by our handsome valet. Perhaps James caught Margo once, though I did not see as much. Now I can see James outside the window with a load of wood for the kitchen. Why, I've seen him carry a load as heavy as a person with not a bit of strain or bother. He, I dare say, splits and stacks cords of wood with the same ease I might exert to split a biscuit for tea.

On Christmas Eve, James brings in a live tree for Laura and me to decorate. I saw as much in *Godey's Lady's Book*. I hear the Queen of England has one this year and since it is a German tradition, Father consented to us having our own in the parlor. We string popped corn and fashion large bows of silk to tie on the branches. Christmas carolers see it in our window and are encouraged to stop at our home. One evening Laura and I join the carolers, though we do not stay out long, merely singing at several homes we know along Chestnut Street. Most evenings we spend around our own piano. Aunt Eliza has taught me to play a new song, but I am not ready to provide a performance, beyond the company of my father's sisters and brother. Of course, I do play for Grandmother Andrews whenever she requests. I do not know if she hears conversations very well, but she can certainly hear music, and joins in singing with no hesitation.

Festivities ebb and flow for days between Christmas and New Year's. Father uses the occasion of the New Year to give gifts to each person in the family. He selected each one with great care and wraps them in silk scarves or handkerchiefs, though I think the graceful knots are made by Aunt Eliza, and I expect she places them on the tree as if they were another decoration.

I receive a leather-bound journal and it is the most beautiful book I have ever seen. It has my own initials, M.E.A., pressed into the corner of the cover. To Joe, he gives a bottle with a small sailing ship inside. My goodness, I do not know how they ever got the ship to fit in the bottle. Father says they build them like that! We are all in grand spirits throughout the holy days – except Joe. I do not know what the matter is with Joe. He has such melancholy, at even the most joyous of times. Laura received a new hat and a muff made of the softest rabbit fur. She has been wearing them in the house every day since she received them.

I knit Father a sweater. It is the largest project I have ever accomplished, and I am glad I began in the summer, when the New Year seemed so far away, for it was not completed until just a few days after Christmas.

I began knitting a muffler for Edward, soon after I finished his slippers, but it remains unfinished today! Father's sweater took much more time than I had imagined, and of course, I did not dare work on something for Edward once his letters stopped. It would have been completely improper for me to give him a gift when one was not expected in return. Now, I do wish I could see him and have any type of exchange. I do not know how he has enjoyed his holyday, since I have had no word from Liz since her departure. I expect that this will not be one he wishes to look back upon with fond memories.

My own party is held just three days into the New Year to which I invite several neighbors. I keep the tree decorated for my party, adding braided cords of gold and red silk threads. We do not believe it is 1851!

Tomorrow I will take the decorations off the tree and James will remove it from the parlor to be planted in the spring. Winter has settled upon Salem. I wonder how Edward fares in the remote little town of Warren, and I wonder if he thinks of me. Just in case he has forgotten about me, I will write and share about my family's holyday and send him my best wishes for his new year.

II. Quaboag Seminary

Edward was expected to follow in his father's footsteps and pursue a law degree, yet Edward's professors implied he might be well suited to become a minister or professor.

Quaboag Seminary, Warren, Massachusetts

CHAPTER 6

—•┅─────•⟨∞⟩•─────┅•—

The Birds in Hartford

Miss M. Lizzie Andrews,
Care of Col. Joseph Andrews,
Salem,
Massachusetts.

Warren – [Tuesday] February 25 - 1851

My dear cousin,

Today closes a short recess of one week, which I have passed very pleasantly with my old friends at Hartford, and which has deferred my writing to you for several weeks; for I thought I might be better able to interest you by waiting till after my vacation, although I desired to answer your last letter during the first of the month.

Allow me, here, my dear cousin to thank you heartily for your frank and kind remarks concerning myself in your last letter, and to assure you that they will ever be respected and always cherished as a momento of your kindly feeling towards me and of your interest in my welfare. To your good wishes I would add my own determination and trust the future may have less reason to complain of my waywardness and lack of resolution.

The winter term of Quaboag Seminary closed on Tuesday of last week and as my teachers were to be absent from Warren, I obtained Father's consent to visit the Birds and pass a few days amid the scenes of my former sports and study. I left our little village on Wednesday morning and in a few hours had reached the old "Pavilion" within the wings of whose happy inmates I met with hearty welcome.

Everything seemed perfectly natural and unchanged since my departure, and at first every face I met was the same as ever. Even old Tony, the Maltese servant was there and when he saw me he threw his arms around me and in his broken English welcomed me back to Hartford. "Ina glad uite come back; uite great man now; smilie like you' fader" &c were from him the words of hearty rejoicing at my return. But when I entered the school house and looked around to discover the well known forms of my companions and schoolmates, I looked in vain and among that row of twenty cheerful faces one only was familiar. All the others were new and unknown and yet I thought I still found a resemblance in some and that they were the same, strangely altered. But no; one alone was there; the others had separated to meet no more; scattered throughout the country, they were all pursuing the course in Life, which had been marked out for them, and most of them I should never see again; one had died; another had left the country: some were at the South, some in Canada and but three or four were near to Hartford.

(I must not indulge in gloomy reflections, and yet as I think of the great changes a few short years will effect, I can scarce refrain.) The boys told me they have fine times there now, and when they return home for a short vacation are all desirous to shorten their holydays and even commence school again rather than be absent from Hartford.

Mr. Bird has five horses, all of them excellent saddle horses and the scholars enjoy riding very much, of which in summer they have sufficient.

I remained at the Pavilion during the extent of my vacation and was very sorry to leave this morning. The visit seemed to me very short and I almost wished I were to attend school there once more, and pass more days as happy as "those of yore." But it was my father's wish that I should return at the commencement of the term and therefore my duty to be punctual.

Upon reaching Warren this afternoon, I found a letter from Albert Browne of Salem making mention of a party at your house he was to attend and expressing a wish that I were to be present. I wish so too, and much would I have enjoyed making you a visit, were it possible. But I shall not (probably) visit Salem for some time yet, much as I desire so to do; you will remember what I told you at Hamilton and since then a circumstance has occurred which ought to prevent my soon appearing where the change in my condition is so well known.

When you write to me I should be very much pleased to receive an account of your soiree and of the doings and actions upon that important occasion. What characters that I know, figured prominently? Who made your Sponge Cake and lemon creams? Was any one before hands with JW this time, as a certain white headed youth was about a year ago? In fine, did you have a pleasant time? I should also have liked very much to have peeped in upon you "New Year's eve," and seen the beautiful gifts ready to drop from your tree, arranged, I know, with a certain charm and a taste always so pleasing.

But I have not yet told you anything about Warren and the school which is to be my residence till August.

To begin – I will say that I am perfectly charmed with the place, and shall not attempt to give any description of its numerous beauties (I mean of scenery) but only tell you what it is, viz. a delightful little village, situated upon a charming little stream, and surrounded on all sides by high and shady hills, which afford places for beautiful walks and extension views. If I could

70

write a description, I would send it to you; if I could paint or draw you should have immediately a sketch of Warren and then I know you would long to visit the place and realize true pleasure, that is, if you are fond of such beauties. I do wish that you were to stay here a short time and we could walk each day to the summit of one of these woody mountains and (if you were attending the Seminary) study our lessons together. - But I must not build castles in the air with such poor hopes of their reality. You will excuse me, I know.

My acquaintances have been very pleasant and I do not anticipate that my short stay in the place will be at all disagreeable. In the Seminary (which is called Quaboag) there were last term about fifty scholars, one half female, and as I only spend a short portion of each day at the Academy, I was obliged to associate with those only whom I chose. Each term continues eleven weeks so that my next vacation will come in May; I do not yet know whether I shall then return to Methuen or not.

Does Joe attend school this winter? He owes me a letter which I should be very happy to receive at his earliest convenience, that is if he is disposed to continue our correspondence, which he seems trying to break off; I hope that he will not for a moment entertain such a thought but will write to me again, and I should be very happy to have an opportunity of writing to him without seeming to crowd upon his attention something which he may perhaps not desire.

I would not have you think, my dear cousin, that Albert Browne is one of my correspondents; the letter I received from him today is the first communication between us, and which I shall answer in course of a week or two. He will return to Cambridge at the same time with myself and very naturally feels the want of a little sympathy, since we knew each other very well in college, and circumstances placed us together a good deal although we were never intimate. I learn from Aunt

Sprague who is now staying with Carrie, that Browne studies very well, and I hope his lesson may prove beneficial as well as my own. I think he has changed very much within a few years and there are many points in his character that I like very much. He means to do well and tries to make friends of all his associates and classmates.

JW is not to study a profession, (as perhaps you know) but will devote himself to "Scientific" pursuits. I like J.W very much and was extremely glad to hear from his mother that your Joe was passing considerable of his time in his company.

I wish I could have attended your party on Wednesday evening and enjoyed myself as I know I should had I been present. I shall expect from you a long account of it as you know I shall be very much interested in it. You must excuse me, dear cousin, for writing such a horrid long letter but I couldn't say any less, and have not yet written one half I could tell you and would like to; but I have already occupied too much of your time with reading my nonsense and will postpone all further remarks till my next letter, unless you send me word to stop immediately. I hope that you never permit anyone to know the contents of my letters, as I write for your ears alone and would feel extremely mortified to learn that anyone else had ever perused them. Do, pray show this or any one of them to no one, and you will greatly oblige me. I shall expect to hear from you soon and must close now. Give my love to all (I do not mean give away all my love) and believe me ever

Your brother (not cousin only)
Edward J. Tenney

--------·⟨∞⟩·--------

I read Edward's letter in my own room with as much joy as I felt reading his first letter—no, more joy, for I held out hope of receiving this letter whereas the first was unexpected! Upon absorbing its contents, I subsequently proceeded downstairs to find my brother sitting in the parlor by the window. Sheets of paper were strewn haphazardly across the top of the oak library table. Joe hunched over the table, his shoulders and back rounded like an umbrella. His feet, lifted from the rug, wrapped around the legs of his chair. He concentrated—his tongue, poked slightly out of the corner of his mouth, moved in rhythm with his pen as he dipped it in the ink bottle and then slowly, calculatingly pulled it across his paper. I could see he was not writing a letter. I waited until he completed drawing his line and lifted his pen before I spoke.

"Joe?" I tried to get his attention. No response. I watched and waited. His pen was full again, ready to hit the paper. I stepped closer and spoke up, trying not to startle him.

"Joe, Edward wrote me a letter. He asks if you are in school."

He looked up slowly, raising only his head. His expression was blank. I continued, "I do not know what to tell him."

"Tell him what you will." He dropped his head back to his paper, and continued drawing.

"Joe, I will inform him that you have left school, but I feel I must offer some explanation."

"Why must you?" He did not look up.

"If I do not, he will be left wondering, and possibly think you encountered a situation similar to his own."

"Perhaps I have."

"Joe, you were not captured by the police and taken to the President of your school for suspension." I said, a bit too hotly. I needed to get his attention. He put down his pen, sat up, took a breath, and with a slight but fading smile, began to speak loudly and dramatically.

"I was trapped like an animal. I was told sit quietly, rigid like a rock, lay my hands still, until I was called upon to write or recite. I was told to listen intently, while great scholars poured volumes of ancient knowledge in archaic languages into my ears, and then demanded I deliver it back in the precise pattern they had dished it out. Nonsense, I say.

Utter pooh. I shall not study topics that hold no interest to me, and with which I see no application that provides any promise to my life nor any relevance to my future."

With that, Joe seemed to run out of steam. I was quiet. He continued in a lower tone, head down, "I have no future, Lizzie. Everyone knows that. Why do you not see it?" he demanded. "I am a failure, a total and utter failure. You can tell that to Edward, though he already knows it, but you can articulate it once again. You can spell it out boldly in your letter. There is no f-u-t-u-r-e for Joe. He is not to study a profession," he cupped his hand and methodically waved it across the table, as if he were reading a headline. With that, he capped the ink, rose from his chair, turned slowly and left the room.

I stood stunned, as if I had awoken from a bad dream and needed to find my bearings. I tried to recall all that Joe had said, so I could correspond appropriately with Edward, but all I could remember was Joe's declaration that he had no future. Before I took a step, Aunt Eliza entered the parlor.

"What is it, Lizzie? You look like you have seen a ghost."

"I fear I have, Aunt Eliza. The ghost left only a moment ago. He looked like Joe, and his voice was like Joe's, but I felt I was speaking to someone wholly other."

"What did he say?" she inquired.

I told her as much as I could remember, explaining that I was to return a letter to cousin Edward, but did not know what excuse to make for Joe, for Joe leaving school this winter, for Joe not writing.

"There is no excuse for Joe." Aunt Eliza said matter-of-factly. "There is none needed. He is to be our family's wonder. You need not worry yourself with trying to explain your brother to anyone, Lizzie. He will speak to Edward himself when he is able."

"But Aunt Eliza," I complained, "Joe leaving school is utterly humiliating to Father and to our family."

"No 'buts'," Lizzie. That is no way for a lady to speak." Then in a softer tone, she added, "Pay no concern to what others may think and do not take this on yourself, Lizzie. Say what you wish to your cousin, but speak for yourself only and let Joe speak for himself. That is how you can respect and care for your brother. And for your family. And yourself."

<hr/>

8 March 1851

Joe leaving school is not at all like Edward's departure from Harvard. My brother's circumstances are completely contrary. His departure has no basis in a moral purpose, as does Edward. I worry what is to become of him.

I penned a letter to Edward warning him Joe is simply not one to write. Joe struggles so with the task, having no flair for putting his thoughts on paper – his dramatic "flare" is completely other, I dare say! That is not to say he is utterly inarticulate when someone is in his presence and the thespian in him comes to life. Sadly, he struggles to craft letters.

Salem Latin and High School: Oliver Primary School,
Salem, Massachusetts

15 March 1851

My goodness, I fear Albert Browne wrote Edward on account of my asking him so many questions about Edward. When I learned Albert now studies in Salem, I invited him to my recent celebration of St. Valentine. With Edward at Quaboag, and unable to attend, I welcomed the opportunity to speak of Edward with one of his chums. Nevertheless, I expected Albert would enjoy the company of Laura and her friends as he is not much more than her in age.

Albert's dismissal from Harvard, along with Edward and his chum Dorsheimer, could have turned them in completely other directions so I was pleased to hear both Edward and Albert will return to Harvard, although that is not the fate for Dorsheimer; I wonder what is to become of him now. I have seen him but once, yet he makes such a striking impression on everyone he meets, I could never forget him. He stands so tall and proud, and is extremely well-spoken. Why, when he passes, the ladies are immediately taken to conversation about his gallant appearance, and wide, warm smile.

It has been a month since my Valentine's party and I am ready to plan another. I joined Aunt Eliza for tea and broached the subject.

"Have you nothing more demanding of your attention? When I was a girl I enjoyed only one party a year and that was to celebrate my birthday with my family."

Laura entered the parlor. "That is it, Lizzie. Let us plan a party to celebrate your birthday next month when you turn sixteen!"

"Oh dear! Before you go any further, you should talk to your father."

Laura enthusiastically embraced the idea of a birthday party and began pestering everyone in the house until it was known that something was already in the works. Now, we openly decided what festivities would be held.

I do enjoy knowing about such matters as Edward shared concerning JW, although I should think I would have heard such news from my own brother, before receiving an announcement from my dear cousin. Joe and JW carry on quite well together. JW is a curious and warm man, although he is a bit nervous around the ladies. Still, I find his quiet company not at all offensive to my person. He is a blessing to my brother, as they never seem to have any but the most pleasant of conversations. I heard them talking the other day, when they did not know I was just around the corner.

"I have entirely changed my course of study, Joe." That statement from JW caught my attention.

"Hmmm," was my brother's invitation for more conversation.

"I have been pursuing a course of study that focuses on mechanical engineering."

That lifted my brother's head and he asked enthusiastically, "Will you be designing machines?"

"I do not expect that I will design and construct them, but I wish to be involved in the progress I know can be made with the proper development of such advanced inventions. I am not yet certain which opportunities I will encounter."

"There is a great demand for steamer ships and diverse cars that travel on tracks – not pulled by horses, or coal engines, but powered by steam. You are well-disposed to pursue scientific pursuits, such as that."

"The Homestead Act will encourage rugged individuals and modern pioneers to settle the vast territories to the west."

"Men are laying iron tracks across the western territories to Ohio and Indiana now, and will reach California someday."

"Yes, the race is from both coasts to see who can lay track the fastest. There is furious excitement about transporting goods across this vast land by train. This is such significant progress."

"Clearly they will need to use the newest steam engines to reach all the way to the frontier. They cannot carry coal enough to feed the furnace fires across those entire prairies. Maybe I could draw the design…"

My brother's voice faded into a mumble and I could no longer hear any response. The two walked directly in front of me as I sat on the landing of the stairs, but neither noticed. I could picture a long train of cars, perhaps transporting silks Father acquires to the wealthy gold miners' wives in San Francisco, California. Steam engines. Imagine that, no black soot to trail behind the trains, and no sparks to dust silk dresses or outer cloaks with holes—that is a dread of which I have been told to be wary, and is the most serious problem I find with my travel to Hamilton.

---

18 March 1851

I wish Edward was to attend school in Salem now, or I in Warren, but my wish is not to be. I told him that if he became a teacher, I would be his student, but of course, he would have to teach in Salem, for my own convenience. For now, my studies have resumed in Hamilton, so I must not yearn for something other.

I would have enjoyed a visit from Edward during the past two months, but he would have been faced with explaining the sensitive events that occurred at Harvard to those who have no particular need to know. People want to hear these matters for purely entertainment's sake. I applaud Edward's honesty, but he must not feel obligated to disclose more than he chooses. Yet, his nature is to please people and limiting his discourse is difficult for him. This is the reason people find him so charming and inform him of personal matters, such as those he speaks of now in his letter. I know he was not witness to a bit of it. The scene occurred last year, and was one I had hoped to erase from the memory of every person present—just as Edward would like to erase the scene of his dismissal from Harvard.

The setting for the scene was a small gathering in our home of perhaps ten or twelve persons, mostly my own friends and neighbors near my age, with the addition of Laura's two young lady friends. Aunt Eliza was in the house. Father was in Boston.

My brother felt compelled, as the older brother, to chaperone all the ladies, and there was an occurrence in which Leverett brushed his hand upon Rose Lee's skirt. Joe took it as his duty to confront Leverett.

"I will have to escort you to the door if you continue to intrude upon the ladies as you do," he said standing next to Leverett, looking him directly in the eye. Rose Lee stepped back.

Leverett gave Joe a curious look, seemingly unaware of any precipitating behavior.

Joe continued, "I saw you dare to place your hand upon the lady's waist."

"I did no such thing. I offer Miss Lee the greatest respect. Furthermore, what I did, or did not do, is not a matter of yours, Joe."

By this time every eye was on Joe and Leverett. I averted my eyes and attempted to cause a distraction elsewhere, but Joe's voice became loud and deep and he upstaged my futile attempt.

"I am the man of the house at this moment, Mr. Saltonstall, and in my father's absence, I am responsible for the decorum of my sister's gentlemen guests."

Leverett was not tolerant of this intrusion, and turned to Rose Lee, "Please excuse me while I step outside, and please excuse," he paused, "the behavior of Mr. Andrews." He turned his back on Joe and walked to the door, snatching his coat off the hall tree and opening the door. Then he stood there. Rose Lee quickly led the entire party out of the parlor and into the foyer. It was almost as if a reception line had formed, for Joe, realizing that the door had not been closed, marched along the row of guests to confront Leverett once again. As Joe reached the hall tree, Leverett was out the door and down the street with such a pace as Joe had no chance to catch him.

I was completely embarrassed! I know not in the least why Joe behaved in such a manner. All present could see Leverett was a gentleman, and it was my brother who was out of hand. Much to my dismay, that scene was the thrill of the party for the guests. I do not know why people are drawn so to look on others when they suffer, rather than turn their gaze out of respect.

There is no reason to know someone's misfortunes. The news bulletins contain enough news of death and disaster. I can barely read a page; I so much prefer reading what is new in *Godey's Lady's Book*! I am not surmising that the incident at my party, or even Edward's dismissal, would ever be printed in a bulletin, but spread of such gossip would be a most unpleasant occurrence for our families. So, one best not speak a word to mere friends for, should they inform their mothers or fathers, could a story be told in many social circles. Oh, horror! Even innocent matters can be presented as scandal. That is precisely why I suggested Edward say his "letters from Lizzie" are from his sister. No, not to deceive, but since our news is no concern of anyone other.

<hr />

21 March 1851

I wrote Edward this morning after reading his letters again, as I do every Saturday to savor the experience of our visits.

Edward's visit to the Birds marks the passing days of youth gone by. Oh, to behold one's past through new eyes, for he was but a child of eleven when he began his stay in the Birds' residence. I expect Rev. Bird feels much like his second father, Mrs. Parker as his mother, for he has told me the Birds' children gave him a brother to look up to, but too many sisters to answer to! His extended family must feel much as the Chestnut Street ladies are to me.

My concern for my neighbors grows this year, as the spring weather has not yet warmed out the winter's ill on my street. When Rose Lee's household took ill, Dr. Holyoke declared the illness influenza, *not* cholera or something worse, which brought much relief to everyone concerned, for two years ago death from cholera was everywhere. As soon as illness started this winter, Father changed my plans.

"Lizzie, you are not to continue to board in Hamilton, during these worst winter months. You must arrange with Miss Ward for tutoring, so you may continue your studies in Salem."

"Yes, Father." I uttered the only appropriate response.

"You are needed here. Travel in winter months can expose you to too much cold and wind, Lizzie, so I have decided you shall stay here.

Mr. Lee's household has been severely afflicted this winter. You are to look in on the Lees from time to time."

"Yes, Father." I knew their cook took ill, although I understood she was able to prepare meals for several days before she staid to her bed.

Father explained, "Two of the Lee daughters are abed with fevers and all sort of ailments."

"Bring them soup and remedies as you see fit to help ease the burden on the family. Consult Aunt Eliza as she may have some helpful herbs you can use from our root cellar. You need not go every day and you are not to go inside. I spoke with Emily's brother, Dr. Oliver. He advised us to stay outside the Lee home until their problems are past."

"So I am only to bring it to the door?"

"Yes. The doctor warned you could catch illness upon contact, so simply deliver what you prepare and refuse any offer for tea or conversation. Lizzie, this arrangement is better for them, and better for you. Wash your hands thoroughly with lye soap upon your return. Ask for Rose Lee. She is prepared to treat her family."

"Yes, Father." I replied, thinking it was a remarkable bit of fancy to think an illness could fly about a room and be caught. I must respect Father's warning, though I hope no one suspects I have accepted such superstition! Aunt Eliza was very generous in providing burdock, purple coneflower, licorice and peppermint, the latter to make a more palatable tea, plus cayenne, which she manages to grow indoors in the kitchen since it needs such a warm climate to thrive, and white willow to use only if one holds down food well but fever persists.

---

27 March 1851

Margie Phillips' brother has fallen ill and my own brother says he is also but I see no outward signs of it, though he sleeps most of the day, seeming to conveniently neglect his duties. Aunt Eliza says to mind myself and do as I am told so as to let Joe rest. Margie's situation seems serious. She tells me the doctor has been to see her brother twice for bloodletting. Perhaps I should provide them herbs, and advise her to wash her hands! Oh, I should not speak with such irreverence, but I simply cannot see how one's fate could pass through the air to be caught by another! But, enough already, I must to bed. A good bloodletting and purgative herbs can cure nearly any ailment and set the body back to balance.

***

6 April 1851

I have just returned from a visit with Aunt Mary and my little cousins in Chelsea, after I know not how long since my last visit. The dear ones have advanced so in age since I saw them last: Charles is seven, Louisa five, and Edward three. Aunt Mary is with child again. She likes the name Elizabeth. Would it not be grand were she to name a daughter Elizabeth? With Edward as an older brother, they could be called Little Ned and Little Lizzie! She carries the baby low, however, so says she may bring forth a boy.

The Fellows' children are most active, although they try hard to obey their mother—their fidgeting and squirming cannot be restrained by even the most stiffly starched clothes for they are bursting with life. I see why Aunt Mary urged Father to send me to assist while she is confined to home. I do believe all the demands on me for caretaking have helped me escape any ailment this spring. Perhaps I simply moved too fast to catch them!

If only Edward and I could have entertained and educated the children together, what a grand time we would have had! He is so patient with his little sisters and brother, and it seems so long since I have seen or heard from Edward. The weather is still cold and there is snow on the ground in the dark, shady places; but we are having days of great sunshine and I think winter will melt away soon. Oh, how I yearn for a nice walk in the sun to come upon crocus petals bursting from the frozen ground. Children aside, my true longing is for any sort of outing with Edward as my escort, where we can speak of the events of this long winter. He should be home to Methuen soon for a short vacation in the Tenney household. Certainly Father would consent to my going as well, should I have the pleasure of receiving such an invitation. With this, I began a lengthy missive to mon chere cousine and enjoyed a brisk walk to post it immediately.

CHAPTER 7

Speaking French

Learning Latin provided scholars with a basis in language roots and meaning, not only for medical or legal professions, but also for becoming fluent in the Romance languages, including French and Spanish.

Miss M. Lizzie Andrews
Care of Col. Jos. Andrews
 Salem
Mass.

Warren [Saturday] April 19 - 1851

Dear Lizzie,

I can not resist the temptation to have a short chat with you immediately, although I have just received your letter, and perhaps you would prefer that I should allow a short interval to elapse before answering it. It seems to me an age since I last wrote to you, and I began to entertain the opinion that all recollection of myself was obliterated from your memory and that you had entirely forgotten that such a personage as "Cousin Edward" yet breathed the vital air. But I could not believe that and the last letter from my "sister and cousin Lizzie" convinced me that I was very wrong to begin to ever think so.

I am delighted to hear of your pleasant visit in Boston and Chelsea and could only wish that I had been in Cambridge at the time and enabled to transform my thought's invisible companion into something real and visible. You can not have forgotten the visit you made in Chelsea at the time of the Bunker-Hill celebration, and the ride around Chelsea you took; certainly, I still retain some recollection of the circumstance and of being told by Joe, on our return, that we would kill the horse.

I am very sorry that Joe does not attend school and it causes me additional pain that I must reproach myself with being, in part, the cause of his leaving. When I visited Salem, a year ago I think, Joe was with Mr. Carlton, and there seemed to have commenced a fondness for study, which I hoped would continue and increase with time; but on account of my arrival he left school for one week and has not since rejoined his classes.

Therefore I can but think that had I remained at Methuen, he would still be pursuing his studies and preparing himself for coming life. You will say that after what I have evinced myself, I should be the last of all persons to preach against neglect of duties, but my own experience has led me to pay more attention to myself, to review my past conduct and has convinced me how many and how great advantages I have neglected and how many opportunities for improvement I have scorned.

Do you find any wild flowers, as yet, in Salem? There are bushels of the "Trailing Arbutus" in Warren and I wish you were here to make me a bouquet. And then the walks are charming; I know that you would enjoy them. There are beautiful groves of every kind of tree, and extending in every direction, with paths and avenues through all; there are hills and mountains from whose tops some dozen of the distant villages are visible, and commanding views of hills in New Hampshire and Connecticut as well as of those upon the western border of Massachusetts. From the summit of one hill within an hour's walk can be seen, with a spy-glass, villages forty miles from Warren, and overlooking the tops of Mts. Tom and Holyoke, we see distinctly far beyond.

How do you succeed in French, and in what book are you reading? Perhaps you have advanced far beyond my comprehension, and perchance have already perfected yourself in that language, while I progress very slowly, reading now La Fontaine's Fables, which is interesting and not very difficult. I shall expect a letter from you in French before long, which I think I could translate, and will then try to reply in the same tongue, but will send at the same time in English what I intend to convey in French for fear that otherwise you can not comprehend my jargon. Perhaps it will be more polite for me to make the first attempt myself and therefore I will try and say a few sentences in French, which it will not harm you if you do not understand. Please don't criticize it, for I will acknowledge it to be all wrong.

Je pense, chere cousine, que vous ne me comprissiez pas touchant le montrant de mes lettres, mais le besoin d'espace ne me permettra pas de vous douner des explications a` present. Saus doute, je n'ai pas des objections a` faire, s'il vous plait a` les montrer. Je ne pense pas que je puisse vous voir a` Salem pour long temps, quoique je le desire beaucoup. En trois semaines, je reviendrai chez moi, et vraisemblablabemen je resterai a Methuen pendant un peu de jours. I can not write such "lingo" any more, but must express in "King's English" what I have to say. I may possibly come to Salem to have my teeth attended to, but think it is very doubtful.

You will write to me again before long I know, will you not?

I should have enjoyed your party very much indeed had I been with you at the time. I am sorry Joe could not be induced to be present with the others and have aided you as hostess(?). I write some compositions for the school occasionally and I wish you could see some of them. I will show them to you some time, if I retain possession of them and do not forget it. I am writing some chronicles now which would amuse you.

My home will be much pleasanter next term than it has been since my teacher is to be married during vacation and a very pleasant lady, it is, too, who will become Mrs. Kimball.

I wish that you could visit Methuen in four weeks from now, when I shall probably be at home. Can you not do so? Good bye, for a short time.

Your affectionate brother
Edward

Translation of French passage:

I think, dear cousin, that you might not understand the meaning of my letters but space will not permit giving you the explanation at present. Without doubt, I have no objections to make, please point them out. I do not think that I would be able to see you at Salem for some time, although I would like to very much. In three weeks, I will return home, and probably I will stay in Methuen for a few days.

Edward wrote to me on my sixteenth birthday. How delightful to imagine, be it true or not, he actually remembered it was a celebratory day for me. His letter caused me quite a chuckle, nearly laughing aloud, I was so happy to hear from him in any language! At our last rendezvous he recited several phrases to me in French, and his pronunciation was rather exquisite, but he does not advance nearly as smoothly with his written expression, grammar and syntax. Why, even I can detect that. Shocking!

⚬

3 May 1851

Most years, by the time the tulips and daffodils are in bloom, as they are now, people are feeling quite spry and I am pleased to return to Hamilton.

In reading Edward's last letter once again on the train to Hamilton, I am reminded of our carriage ride last year in Chelsea. I had never before ridden in a carriage without my father, or some other adult. Oh, the fun we had. I recall it as if it were yesterday. I close my eyes and let the rumble of the train lull me into reliving my memory of Edward at the Bunker Hill Celebration.

"Lizzie, your father has asked me to be your guide for the Bunker Hill Celebration," Edward says as he enters Uncle John's dining room, where I am finishing morning tea with Aunt Mary. She looks up and Edward addresses her, speaking so rapidly he nearly trips over his tongue. "The Colonel is going on ahead early with others and I am to take you and Laura in the carriage."

"Have they departed so soon?" Aunt Mary inquires and rises from the table, looking toward the front door. "Please excuse me," she smiles absently, and with tea cup in hand, steps into the kitchen.

Father has not joined us for tea. Being anxious to converse with my uncles about the day's events, he went immediately to greet them in the library upon our arrival. Edward stands by the table, looking at me intently. I realized he expects a response. From me.

"You are to take us?" I ask, smiling. "Oh, that will be grand, Edward. Is Laura ready to depart?"

"In actual fact, Lizzie, Laura says she does not feel up for another carriage ride, having just arrived from an hour of jostling in the carriage from Salem." He pauses, and I can see he is not terribly concerned about Laura. He seems rather excited to have a chance to drive the horses, and continues, "Do you feel fine for such an outing?"

"Oh yes, by all means." I spot my sister reclining on the chaise lounge in the parlor. "Laura must be terribly unsettled from the ride," I concur. I look around for my brother, to no avail, and safely ask aloud, "Will Joe be joining us?"

"I informed Joe that your father requested I escort you two young ladies and I invited him to join us," Edward explains, "but he simply did not answer."

Edward heads to the carriage house to see if the horse is harnessed and hitched to the buggy, as I move toward the front porch to await him. He helps me onto the seat and we are on our way. As the horse rounds the corner, I glance back to see Joe step off of the front porch.

"There is Joe," I said.

"Shall I turn back so he may accompany us?" Edward asked.

Joe merely stands there, with no gesture to bid us to return or farewell.

"I do not think he knows what he wishes to do, Edward. I say we continue. We both know my observation to be a true reflection of what occurs when Joe is in a melancholy state, and not likely to meet the day with good cheer."

Once the troubled memory of Joe left our minds, we found no trouble celebrating each other's company, and yes, also the 75th Anniversary of the Battle of Bunker Hill. Father commanded a very large military escort of four companies of Artillery and five of Infantry to the ship house at the Navy Yard where the British troops landed in Charleston.

After the festivities, the late afternoon filled with sounds of the carriage squeaking and hooves clipping in hollow percussion. The sky seemed to glow an entirely new hue of blue and the sea reflected it back to brighten the sky surrounding the sun. Our horse's rhythmic breathing, in time with each step, announced our arrival to the Starlings, Jays, and Robins, which chirped as we passed them. Seagulls squawked their signature call. The flash of white prompted me to instinctively grab my hat to keep from losing it. As we ventured further, mock orange was fragrant along the streets.

"Are you warm enough, Lizzie? You did not bring a shawl, and I did not think to put an extra blanket in the carriage."

"Edward, the sun is glorious and it is still a beautiful day."

"That it is, Lizzie." He smiled and added, "As are you."

I fell silent. Oh, why does not my mouth reveal the tenderness I feel? I hope he did not interpret my comment about the sun as a disregard of his kind gesture to provide a coverlet for my comfort.

"Edward, have we time to stop and pick flowers?" I said, as we passed a field of lupine, daisies, and columbine.

"That is one thing we have in abundance, Lizzie," he said as he pulled to the side of the road and whoa'd Bobby to a standstill. He wrapped the reins tautly around the brake lever and pressed on the brake with such force that I nearly slid forward off the bench. Edward did not see this, for he was already on the ground, soothing the horse as he passed in front of him. He reached his hand toward me—long before he was close enough for me to grasp it. Once I did, he pulled me toward him with undue force, nearly knocking me fully into himself. He placed his other hand on my waist to keep me from falling and held it there until both my feet were firmly on the ground. I wanted the moment to last forever. I looked up directly into his smile. He looked quickly away. I turned to see where he was looking and his lips quickly met my cheek with a soft kiss. I dared not turn back toward him.

"Come, Lizzie," he said, as he spun to face the field, presenting his elbow toward me. I laid my hand in the crook of his arm and stepped after him. I took but three or four steps when I felt the uneven ground would not allow me to keep his pace. My fingers slid up his arm leaving their easy resting place, and I held tight to keep my footing. I could feel the warmth of his arm through his jacket sleeve. His arm was wider than my fingers could encompass. I had never thought Edward to have such a physique—my musings distracted me from my task of walking. The grasses and flowers were as tall as my waist and though my skirts brushed them out of my way, I could not see past their fullness to where

91

my feet would step. Grasses sprang up inside my skirts as I walked and thorns on the wild tea roses began to snap up under my skirts and snag my bloomers! "Oh my," I emitted, before I realized my mouth had launched its tongue again.

"Are you alright, Lizzie?"

"Oh yes, but I fear I must not go on for the ground is likely to pull me toward it if I make one careless step."

"Stand completely still then," Edward said, as he busily gathered two or three of every color flower he could see. "I will carry your bouquet back to the carriage for you." He took my hand with his free one—his grip firm, warm, his skin soft—and he led me safely from the field.

I held the bouquet on my lap as we continued on our way.

"Hamilton," the conductor called and the train stopped hard, jarring me from my seat with no one to catch me as I slid to my feet and stepped lively to keep my balance.

I will forever remember the grand 75th anniversary celebration of the Battle of Bunker Hill, not for setting the Revolution in motion, however. My memories will be of Edward's strong and tender hands holding daisies, bouquets and me.

CHAPTER 8

A Fish Out of Water

Quaboag Seminary in Warren, Massachusetts was about the same distance to Edward's home in Methuen as it was to Harvard. The trip would have taken about three hours by train in 1850.

Miss M. E. Andrews
Care of Col. J. Andrews
Salem
Mass.

Methuen, [Friday] May 16, 1851

Dear Lizzie,

I fear that you will scarcely know your scribbling cousin, when he attempts to write to you from home. I have very much the sensations of "a fish out of water" and doubt not I shall find myself unable to write one page from this new abode. I always make a rule to neglect all correspondents during vacation, and thus far I have rigidly conformed to my resolution. But I must break it this once, and trusting that my disobedience will be pardoned, shall try in future to "mind the rules."

Of course you can expect no French this time, but you may be sufficiently puzzled to translate what I call "English."

On Wednesday morning I left little Warren and in three hours had joined my mother in Boston, where we remained till five o'clock engaged in dining, shopping &c &c. At six I was in Methuen kissing and shaking hands with a host of brothers, sisters &c from whom I had been separated five long months. Little Lottie seemed delighted with the return of her "grandfather" and for a long time my arms were loaded with the little ones all. Even now while I am trying in vain to think, my ears are filled with their clatter, my table is shaken and my own person even is not free from their restless hands. Were it any one but Johnny, Margie, Lottie, I believe that I could give them a sound whipping and send them down stairs.

I do not think, dear cousin, that I shall be able to visit Salem during my short vacation. It will close in a fortnight and I ought to remain the whole of the time at Methuen. But I do not intend to remain long at Warren after my return and then perhaps may call at Hamilton for a day or two. I shall rejoin my class in Harvard, the latter part of August and shall leave Warren some six or eight weeks before that time. In July Father will be absent from Methuen, and during a great portion of my vacation, I shall be needed here to supply his place. Besides Mother has already engaged that I should visit Weathersfield, Vt. and although the promise was made without my knowledge, I should be very happy to fulfil my share of it.

Liz still attends school in Lawrence, and I was very happy to hear that you corresponded with her. Do come and see us if you can. Unless I am mistaken nearly two years have passed since you made your last appearance among the Tenneys and then only for a short time did they have the pleasure of your society.

During that short visit I was at Cambridge nor can I call to mind a single time that you have made us a visit, at least while I was in Methuen. If you do not come now, do not fail, by any means, to make us a long, long visit when your August vacation shall have come.

Eddie Smith you have already seen I suppose, and you must have been delighted to welcome back to Salem the long-lost Carrie. Without her my sojourn at Warren would have been unpleasant and the long terms would have seemed dreary and sad. I do think Carrie Smith is one of the best, pleasantest ladies I ever saw. Until my departure from Cambridge, I hardly knew her, and the little acquaintance I had formed with her, gave me no insight into her character, or no sure knowledge of her excellence. But one week had not passed after I sought Warren, before I was fully convinced that happen what might, my stay would be far from unpleasant, and that I could not be otherwise than happy, while cousin Carrie was near me.

When next I visit Salem I shall expect to see you the quasi-mistress of a splendid mansion on Essex Street as happy and joyous as possible. I am very glad to learn of your father's intention to build this summer, as pleasant for himself and family.

Our garden does not yet appear very gorgeous, though the tulips and hyacinths are in full bloom and several inferior flowers lend their feeble aid to increase the fragrance and beauty of a short promenade. Lottie is "flower" enough for all and everything seems common-place by her side. I do wish you could chat with her for a few moments. The little thing can now talk as well as the best of us and though sometimes you might suppose she was jabbering in French, a little practice would soon accustom you to her "brogue."

Of course I shall not again attempt to write French, and be assured that my last letter should have been destroyed had I attempted my "foreignification" at an earlier period in my epistle. But I did not wish to destroy four pages of my brain merely to avoid being ridiculed for attempting to write what I did not understand. I shall return to Quaboag in two wks. and be back again in July.

How do you like Carrie's baby? A bright little thing he seems, though too small. The Grandfather is charmed with this his first and only grandson, and was caressing him the whole time, while he staid in Warren (two or three days).

Do you attend school in Salem as before or have you made a change? I am very much obliged to you for your prompt letter and would be gratified to hear from you soon again, if convenient for you to write to me. Liz is waiting a letter from you, she says. Mother is not very well today, but will soon recover I doubt not. With the kindest wishes for your happiness, I am ever.

Your affectionate cousin
Ned

----

24 May 1851

Sitting on the front porch with Edward's letter on my lap, I closed my eyes from the brightness of the morning and let my mind fill with the pictures Edward's words had painted. Picture Joseph Sprague, a grandfather; his first grandson softening his heart. Picture Edward's stepmother Augusta arranging a visit for Edward to see his aunt. Our aunts have been so important in our lives. How fortunate we both are that our mothers had so many fine sisters - his, mine, and then ours together. His visit with his mother's sister will be a highlight of his summer I am certain. She will transmit a fondness only someone close to a sister can portray. Picture the voice, the stature, the look of approval. Or, God forbid, the look of disapproval that causes you to stop dead in your tracks. Aunt Eliza has fixed that look on my brother Joe! I cannot imagine Edward's aunt Anna Bailey Bartlett ever donning the

96

look, or her husband, the Honorable William Jarvis. Oh, envy, that I, too, could have a fortnight with Edward! Such a two-week visit would fill me with lasting memories of conversations and entertainments we both so desire.

Sitting uninterrupted, eyes closed, images of Edward and my last visit to Methuen appeared in my mind's view as if presented by stereoscope. Surely, Edward's forgetfulness of my visit is simply a mistake for it was not I who neglected such a visit. It was he who was the cause of us not seeing each other. I dutifully called at the Tenney household last August. As I recall, my sweet cousin had gone to Cambridge by the time I arrived, and though we have spoken of my pleasant visit with my Aunts and young cousins, Edward seems to have put it completely out of his mind in less than a year, as if it had been a century ago that we met. It feels that way to me, too!

Aunt Eliza's voice startled me, "Are you dozing, Lizzie?" I popped to attention to reassure her I was doing no such thing, just resting my eyes after reading.

"Very well then. I am off to the market," she continued on her way. I did not want to see if she was wearing her look as she stepped away.

Rallying myself from idleness, I crafted a message to relay to Edward through his sister Liz, despite my concern she might impress upon him his error without the delicacy I would prefer. I am in receipt of her last letter between us, so am due to write. Surely she remembers it is not I who owes a visit. Quite the contrary, she and Mary are most obliged to call on me next. I shall also write Edward to ascertain whether he thinks they intend to call on me in Salem. Perhaps he can see to it I receive such a visit!

Brushing down the layers of my dress, I rose, wondering if Edward also forgot that I no longer board in Hamilton. I have re-commenced daily travel, being the first in the household to arise, aside from Margo and James, of course. 'Tho I have help dressing, I often take my leave before they have prepared breakfast, for my train departs Salem just as the sun is rising. It is not far to go alone to the depot. If there is no chill in the air, I often walk the few blocks. I prefer to warm my limbs from the very activity, rather than wait for James to drive the carriage. The days are becoming quite warm and bright. Of that, I am supremely gladdened and left the porch with no regret for having indulged the morning sun.

It should be possible for me to make a call to Methuen during my vacation in summer, though not until early in August. August seems to be forever away.

---

28 June 1851

My studies have consumed me. I have advanced in French and German, and enjoyed much time with English literature. I have completed reading the *Scarlet Letter*, by Nathaniel Hawthorn. I think it might be better titled by Shakespeare as Much Ado About Nothing. It is worrisome to me the attention given by some to the affairs of others. Oh yes, society needs to keep a moral order, but who are we to judge another, especially in matters of the heart? Further, how are we to ever know the deep workings of another? Why must we make a public spectacle of others' pain?

I also read in an essay by Ralph Waldo Emerson's *Nature*:

"For the Universe has three children, born at one time, which reappear, under different names, in every system of thought, whether they be called cause, operation, and effect; or, more poetically, Jove, Pluto, Neptune; or, theologically, the Father, the Spirit, and the Son; but which we will call here, the Knower, the Doer, and the Sayer. These stand respectively for the love of truth, for the love of good, and for the love of beauty. These three are equal. Each is that which he is essentially, so that he cannot be surmounted or analyzed, and each of these three has the power of the others latent in him, and his own patent."

My father is a Knower. Edward a Doer... and Sayer. I am but a blank slate upon which the men in my life write. All I am called to do is keep from being soiled with the thoughts and deeds of others.

During a break before the last Sabbath, I enjoyed a short trip to Ipswich for a delightful ride on a majestic old mare. As fine as she was, after but a moment in the saddle, I was ready to dismount. I fear the horse could sense my inexperience, for she responded to my every quiver, and seemed to suspend all movement until I issued a command. But, I was unsure of my own ability to control such a large animal, and imagined she could sweep me away in an instant and at her own whim. I was what seemed a full hour atop the steed when I was informed it had been but half that. I must learn so much to gain confidence my skills would allow me to ride off the estate.

———————

6 July 1851

Liz and Mary have arranged a visit in ten days. I hope they will meet me in Hamilton for I am to continue my studies there until the time they are to arrive. Then, I will take my summer break. Father has arranged for me to make several visits to Ipswich to ride a saddle horse. I am hoping Margie Phillips will join me, for she is quite a skilled equestrian, 'tho she usually does not venture as far as Ipswich to ride.

I wish Liz and Mary could have arrived in Salem for the Fourth of July celebration, and that Edward had made the journey as well.

It was a lovely gathering, throughout the entire evening. We did not expect as much since the rains continued the whole day, as they had for two days prior. The sky was gray until dinnertime, the rains having ceased just before the procession of carriages, so finely adorned – entirely with fresh flowers. Even the horses had blossoms tucked into their bridles and along their saddles.

By supper, the sun broke through and warmed the air, then colored it splendidly on its way down. 'Tho the grounds were quite soggy, the display of stars and fireworks was extraordinary.

We had a grand time—Rose Lee, Margie Phillips, Laura and two other of her friends, all six of us young ladies together with the fullest of skirts and with our parasols to shield us from the drizzle or the sun, as it broke through the clouds intermittently throughout the day. The light rain cleaned the wood smoke from the air and made the foliage glisten and we even saw a glimmer of a faint rainbow overhead during one of the welcomed sun breaks. James brought a blanket to dry a spot for us on a long bench. We sat there in the central square, in a position to see the display with perfect clarity.

We ourselves were a display, however, for Laura seems to know every young man in Salem. We were greeted constantly and by many who came to bid us well. People who know Father addressed us by name in such numbers that I fear we distracted from the purpose of the celebration.

"Greetings Miss Andrews, Miss Andrews," one would nod at Laura and me.

"Good day, Miss Andrews, Miss Andrews. Ladies," another would extend his greeting to our friends. My ears filled with the sounds of these delightful greetings. Of course, Father kept an eye on us like a hawk, but did not seem to mind that so many turned our heads. Why, he himself brought new friends over to us for introductions.

Father certainly has managed to become well acquainted with many. He knows half the town, I expect, and the other half of Salem citizens seem to recognize him!

Joe did not join us, preferring to make preparations for his departure to Methuen. He is to enjoy a lengthy visit with the Tenneys. Oh, how I long for such a visit, which will come in due time for me as well.

I hope to receive soon a response from Edward to my last letter, though he has been quite busy with his studies at Warren through the past month. My own studies will complete in two weeks and Laura and I shall follow Joe's lead to the Tenney's for a visit.

CHAPTER 9

Graduating from Quaboag Seminary

Unlike Edward's earlier college preparatory education at the Bird's in Hartford, Edward lived with his principal at Quaboag and was able to pursue college level studies.

Miss M. E. Andrews,
Care of Col. J. Andrews,
Salem
Massachusetts

Methuen, [Sunday] July 13th 1851

Dear Cousin,

I was mistaken in charging you with having neglected us for so many centuries(!) and I beg your pardon for forgetting your call of last year. Still I hope *that* brief visit will not prevent your coming to Methuen during your next vacation nor that the fact of having made the last call will keep you away, even if Liz or

Mary fail to see you at Hamilton. I do think they will be able to go to Salem at present: therefore you must not wait for them: we all expect you soon.

Since I last wrote to you, my studies at Warren have been completed. I have graduated at Quaboag Seminary (without any suspension this time) and am now trying to enjoy a long vacation. I shall not rejoin my class till August 30th and meanwhile will remain nearly all of the time at Methuen. Even were I disposed to leave home for a few weeks I should not feel willing to do so now. I have company at present, I am expecting a cousin from the South and Liz is on the lookout for yourself and Laura, the entertainment of each and all of whom will afford me as much pleasure as to leave Methuen.

I was gratified by finding Joe here on Friday last and I am very glad that he is to make us a good long visit, unless he becomes homesick or tired of our village. Yesterday afternoon Joe and I, with Aunts Mary (Fellows) and Margaret, drove to Mrs. Bridges in Andover, spent an hour with her and returning about seven o'clock found some girls (I beg your pardon - young ladies) from Lawrence - who had been spending the afternoon with Liz and Mary. As soon as I had deposited one load, I received another and rode to Lawrence, pretty tired of sitting in a carriage though well pleased, of course, with my companions.

How J. and myself shall manage to enjoy ourselves, I can not tell: chess, fishing, sleeping and other intellectual amusements will aid, I hope, our gratification and help to while away the time from day to day. - An interruption compels me to pause here for a short time.

Sabbath eve - I have now, for a wonder, a moment alone and free and I will try to finish my sheet before I again receive a call. I can very seldom be by myself, when at home, long enough to even collect my thoughts, much less for committing them to paper. While I was writing this morning there were three persons in the room (besides myself) all conversing and occasionally asking questions of me, probably to aid me in my letter. Our house, to-day, has been almost full and whoever wishes quiet seeks my room as the farthest removed from noise. At dinner there were 18, at breakfast & supper one less, so that you can imagine what opportunity to be alone one has.

I intended, Liz, to have answered your last letter before now, but various matters have caused me to postpone it a fortnight. I thank you for your invitation to visit Hamilton this summer, but I shall be unable to accept it, though nothing would please me better.

Father and Mother will be absent from home a portion of my vacation and then I can not leave; during the latter part of it I shall remain to entertain guests, yourself among the number, I trust.

I regret that I did not pass the fourth of July in Salem: but I knew the weather was unpleasant and expected there would be no display: that I should become very much fatigued for nothing and that I should derive far greater enjoyment by remaining at home. All who did go assured me they were very much pleased and a description of the floral procession caused me to wish I too had accompanied them. The only display I viewed was the Lawrence fire-works - which was quite good.

Joe tells me that you leave for Hamilton as early in the morning now as when I last saw you. I thought Liz Tenney was away in very good season and she does not start before half past seven. As I write, Joe lies abed before me, and asleep, too, if I am to judge by the sounds occasionally proceeding from his nasal organ.

When I began the latter portion of my letter he was sitting below; but soon found his way to the regions above and "doffing his garments" was soon searching for "Tired nature's sweet restorer" who is calling for me too; and soon I must obey his mandate, if I would be up betimes tomorrow. I pity you as I think of your hurrying to the depot at half past six, minus your breakfast, half awake and shivering with cold.

I suppose you have had plenty of rides with the horses this summer; - how often do you go to Ipswich? I wish I was there to drive you round with Bobby. You have not forgotten that ride from Boston in the evening after the Taylor celebration.

Write soon - be sure to visit Methuen the first week of your vacation and stay as long as you can. We all expect you from small to great. I would ask Joe for any message were he awake; but I'll not trouble him now. I gave Liz your message.

Ever your cousin E. J. Tenney (Remember me to all friends)

---

26 July 1851

Would the Tenneys even notice me if I appeared as one more at the Tenney table? I imagined joining their family of eight, along with Aunt Margaret, Aunt Mary, her three children, Mrs. Bridges, three of her children and my brother Joe. Fathers often came home from work to join the family for dinner at noon. After the large, mid-day meal, they returned to work. How I longed to be there and stay for a lengthy visit. I would even settle for a supper-time visit, though a lighter, less formal meal, being served at the end of the day would allow me to linger through the evening.

Instead, I have been riding horses in Ipswich with Laura, Liz and Mary Tenney. We boarded at the riding school there, and after five days, we could nearly call ourselves equestrians, 'tho everyone seemed to advance more quickly than myself. Remarkably, Liz is already quite accomplished.

The first day, we were schooled in the etiquette of riding style, learning the proper timing, pace, and commands for the horse. Once we could recite what we knew to our instructor's satisfaction, he led us to the stable.

"Liz, have you ridden before?" the stable boy asked my cousin.

"I've ridden just a bit before," she responded and then turning to me continued, "but without a proper riding outfit." She did look smart in her new split skirt and high-top boots that laced in front, 'tho the lacings of course were entirely hidden by her skirt. Her short riding jacket had lacing also. She wore a different hat from the ones Laura and I had. Father had found us outfits with feathers in the hats.

"When did you ride before, Liz?" Laura asked.

"Oh, I was very young. Edward learned to ride when he was living in Hartford. When he came home to Methuen for the summer, Father borrowed a sidesaddle and permitted me to sit in it while Edward led the horse. I rode only in a ring with my brother keeping close watch."

"Imagine if our brother would have shown such kindness to us," I said to Laura.

"I can only imagine," she replied somberly.

The stable boy inquired of me next, and I responded. "The only riding to which I am accustomed is well behind the horse, snugly inside a carriage."

He warned us, "Riding directly atop the horse may be a difficult venture—rougher than you expect. The ladies' sidesaddle demands balance and great skill, but you must not be discouraged if the first time out is difficult."

Our horses were ready—bridled and saddled. He selected one for each of us and helped us mount.

As we strode out of the stable, I feared I would slide deftly from the horse's back to the hard ground at the least provocation. How is it I feel so insecure, I wondered, as I tried to maintain my balance. I soon felt myself slipping further backward and nearly over the side, while I pathetically bent forward—my desperate attempt nearly putting my head in my lap! Oh, how I longed for a saddle with a horn, like they use in the Wild, Wild West shows, so I could grasp on for my dear life!

The stable boy came chasing after me and my horse, but not to urge us onward as I suspected. Instead, he grasped my horse's bridle and stretched his other hand to help me dismount. Before I realized what was happening, I was safely on my feet and he was pushing his knee into my horse's side. I saw that the cinch hung loosely, and the fault lay with my horse, not me.

"Your mare has bloated herself to prevent a secure fit of the saddle. I thought I had her straightened out, but she is a tricky one," he explained, as he took up the slack in the cinch.

"My word," I said, shocked at how easily he knocked the wind out of her. "Such absurd behavior for an animal." Tho' I truly did understand my horse wanting to be free of her snug corset.

Turning, so only my riding companions could hear, I continued, "If anyone tried to snug me in a leather corset and climb on my back, I would object, too." That sent Liz, Laura and Mary into fits of laughter.

Once we were on our way, I tried to ride lightly so as not to burden the beast beneath. Liz told me my face looked rather as if I had seen a ghost and speculated whether I would ever get willingly back on a horse for the pleasure of the ride. I proved her wrong, however.

By mid-week, I settled comfortably into the sidesaddle and could follow the horse's pace. The ride felt quite as smooth as if I were riding in a carriage, perhaps more. This activity demands more strength than I ever imagined, however. My limbs were given to tremble with fatigue by the end of the ride and walking was far from a display of grace.

At the end of the week, I was happy to ride back to Hamilton behind the horse again. We actually cheered when we saw our iron horse pull into the station.

"Riding to Salem in the cars is a welcome treat," I offered.

"For my person, I look forward to my next opportunity to view the world from the heights one achieves atop a horse." Laura countered.

"Perhaps James can set you up to ride Bobby," I suggested, adding "though he is trained to pull our carriage and may not be considered a good saddle horse." Noticing this distinction was an indication I had accomplished at least some understanding of the animal. Like people, some of us are built to pull and drag, others to shoulder a burden directly on their backs … and some resist both, like my brother Joe.

2 August 1851

Shocking news! My brother has gone to McLean Asylum at Somerville. This is a dreadful and sad predicament for Joe. Aunt Eliza tells me his trouble increased after he returned from Methuen. Laura and I were away.

Father did not send for us to return to Salem when Joe went to the hospital, not wishing to shorten our vacation! He says there was nothing anyone could have done to change a thing. I cannot help but wonder if we may have been able to help him bear his burden. We were not witness to what prevailed. Joe's illness caused him to sleep for three full days upon his return from Methuen. Aunt Eliza says he was suffering from melancholy and was completely unable to rally from his bed. She felt no feverish heat from his head; though his eyes would barely open and his breathing was very quiet. His spirits were so low he could scarcely talk to explain what was the matter. Aunt Eliza summoned Dr. Holyoke and Father.

Now, Joe has a most knowledgeable physician named Dr. Bell, who treats conditions like his. The treatment demands he be confined to an asylum! What treatment is this? Perhaps simply the typical bloodletting and immersion bathing? I hear they have indoor bathtubs for treatment.

Somerville is very near Harvard. Father has not yet been allowed to see him. He says there is no reason for me to be concerned although we may not see him for some time. That concerns me! I want to protest to Father. Why can I not see Joe to know he fares well? I regret that I have been so short with my brother, but I did not know there was a true cause to his ill-mannered temperament aside from stubbornness. I promised myself to make every effort to treat him with patience and the utmost kindness, if only I can be forgiven for my impatience and ruthlessness of the past.

Railroad Station, Salem, Massachusetts

11 August 1851

Edward greeted Laura and me at the train station in Lawrence today as we arrived for a summer visit.

When Edward greeted us at the station, I wanted to fly into his arms the moment I saw him. Of course, that would have made a most improper public display. Edward approached us and held my shoulders lightly. He did not touch my cheeks with kisses as he showed the greatest restraint.

The carriage ride to Methuen allowed us to enjoy each other's company with light conversation about the activities of the late summer season and anticipation of departing soon for school. Edward is eager, albeit somewhat apprehensive, for his return to Harvard.

I adore riding in the carriage watching Edward control the horses. We arrive at the Tenney's in time to enjoy afternoon tea with his father, Aunt Augusta and Aunt Margaret. There is much excitement about Uncle John and Aunt Augusta's departure the next morning. After tea, Senator Tenney addressed Edward, "Son, remember, you are to stay home all the time we are away, the only exception being a carriage ride to return Lizzie and Laura to the train station in Lawrence."

"Yes, of course, Father."

Edward follows his father into the library and the rest of their lengthy conversation is lost to me, though I regretted missing a bit of Edward's company now that I was so near. Liz, Mary, Laura and I retreated to the parlor until supper to enjoy each other's company while we looked at the latest *Godey's Lady's Book*. The children clamored sweetly for our attention. We were especially entertained with Lottie's clever antics. It is nearly impossible to take one's eyes off her as she parades about amusing herself with anything within her reach.

After supper, Aunt Augusta carried little Lottie up the stairs, saying, "You be a good girl for Aunt Margaret while mama and papa are away." Aunt Margaret began to rally Johnny and Margie toward bed and they went willingly in hopes of a nighttime story from their dear aunt.

Senator Tenney issued additional instructions to Edward, "Aunt Margaret will see to the care of the children at bed, but should not be bothered with any other household matters during our absence. Those are yours to manage, son. You must act as the head of this household. I am depending on you." The Senator looked at me as he continued, "Please provide any assistance Aunt Margaret might require." I joined Edward in nodding assent, pleased to be included as someone he could depend upon.

Uncle John continued, softening his tone, "Tonight, however, perhaps Laura and Mary will be so kind as to help Aunt Margaret tuck the little ones in bed." Mary and Laura jumped up to follow Aunt Margaret.

Aunt Augusta appeared back downstairs within moments. Soon Edward's father encourages her to retire with him for the evening, leaving Edward, Liz and me in the parlor just as Aunt Margaret returns.

"How is your brother, Lizzie?" Aunt Margaret asks me, as she settles into the rocking chair.

Aunt Margaret has always had particular sympathies for Joe, saying he has special gifts. This makes it very easy to talk to her about my brother for she seems to understand sickness. I relay what Aunt Eliza has told me, both regretting and feeling relieved that I was away when he departed our home.

Seeming to be satisfied that she is now well versed in the family news, Aunt Margaret bids us good night, takes her candle and moves toward the door. She leaves us with the admonition that we not burn the candles to their very end, for we are to be up with the sun to wish Senator Tenney and Aunt Augusta a bon voyage.

Looking directly at Edward, she adds, "I will be assessing the candle length in the morning as a measure of your discipline." Edward's face flushes and fills with seriousness. I glimpse Aunt Margaret's wide smile and she winks at me as she passes. This is quite curious, for she knows nothing of my fond sentiments for Edward. Even Liz is unaware of the true feelings her brother and I have for each other. I must assume

Aunt Margaret's wink to be a reference to the challenges Edward has had after his dismissal from Harvard, rather than any direct implication of my presence. Edward's family certainly demonstrates a fair degree of confidence and trust in him, so it is curious that they would tease him about his challenges. Perhaps Aunt Margaret's wink revealed she sees right through us.

Liz's eyes dart between Edward's and mine as we watch Aunt Margaret depart. To divert Liz's attention, I ask, "Liz, what have you read this summer? Have you finished the book you began reading when we were in Ipswich?"

Confessing she had not, our discourse delved into literature we simply devoured and that which we abhorred, as well as music that sent goose bumps up our limbs. Also, the beauty of nature in the outings we have taken during the summer and, of course, on our rides in Ipswich. Edward has great knowledge of music and the most popular and critically acclaimed performers. Liz and I envied his ability to engage in public appearances as often as he did. The candle began to flicker as the wax diminished. Edward looked to the oil lamp, sitting cold just a foot from the candle, and sighed. Liz shoots him a look as if to say, "You dare not light it."

I broke their loud silence with, "I fear my trip has made me weary and sleep is ready to overcome me. Shall we finish our evening with a passage from the Bible?"

"Yes. Let us. And then I, too, am ready for night's sweet restorer," Edward offers and stands to retrieve the family Bible. He sits between Liz and me as if to share in our gaze on the page. "Shall we do this each night you are here, Lizzie?" he asks. I nod my assent but am at a loss for words as I feel so small next to him and admit to feeling a bit distracted by the proximity of his person. We each read briefly and Edward returns the Bible to the shelf.

Liz stands first, taking a candle in one hand. "Come, Lizzie, we will go up together." She offers her other hand to me.

"I best be to bed as well." Edward stands close by me and bows slightly forward, bidding us good night. He tips a candle to light off

Liz's and follows us up the stairs, heading left at the top step. We head right to Liz's room.

Liz and I are fast to slumber. It seems that only a few minutes pass before morning floods the room and Maree the Irish servant girl is at our door offering to help us dress for breakfast.

"Laydees. Good mor'nun, laydees," she says in her Irish brogue. "Mai aye aelp yers with yer kursetts?" Without waiting for a response, she continues, "The senator and the Missus are at breakfust alruddy."

By the time we have risen to the edges of our beds, Maree has our dresses draped across the footboard of the bed and she is holding Liz's corset for her. Liz turns to face me as Maree wraps the corset around her and tugs at the laces on her back until they are snug.

"Lizzie, does this remind you of your horse in Ipswich?" she begins to giggle, and Maree hushes her. "Lady Liz and now, a new little Lady Liz-E. Aye! Ya are both Liz-Beth! How is a one to know how ta talk ta ya?"

We both enjoy a good laugh as Maree tugs on my corset ties. Soon she is draping our dresses over our heads and inquiring if we can help each other finish from here so she can get the senator and Mrs. on their way. We pull on our own stockings, and button our shoes. Liz and I brush each other's hair, parting it in the middle and pulling it back in a knot at the nape of our necks. My hair falls to my waist in thick waves when it is not tied up. Liz's is nearly as long but darker and sleeker. This is the simple style that all young ladies wear. We rarely bother with the fancy arrangements of curls and ringlets so common to our aunts. Since we both have lost our mothers, our aunts have been mothers to us. Aunt Augusta is the only mother Liz has known. Liz was barely walking when her mother died birthing her sister Mary.

We head for the stairs and descend one after the other, using the handrail as the guide for it is not possible to see our feet under the full-ness of our skirts.

"Aye, here they are now," Maree says as we approach. The Tenney's luggage is in the foyer, and we hear voices in the kitchen. The smell of fresh coffee and biscuits greets us as we approach the table. Soon there are eggs and bacon mingled with the merriment of the Tenneys.

The Senator and Aunt Augusta have not traveled together just the two of them without the children, and have never left Edward in charge before. But, it is time to wean little Lottie, now two and this is a customary way to accomplish that. Senator Tenney's voice exhibits a mix of pride and apprehension as he bids good-bye to his six children, spanning in age from two to seventeen.

The morning consists of helping dress the children for outdoor play and it soon flies by. At noon we are being called to dinner, so begins the washing and dressing of children again, uncovering shining faces from under the dirt and grass stains they have so quickly collected during their play.

Edward sits at the head of the table in his father's chair, and asks the servants, Beth and Maree, to stay in the room while he says grace. They stand quietly by the kitchen door and bow their heads respectfully.

"Heavenly Father, thank you for the meal and for the hands that prepared it. Thank you for keeping us well, and for watching over us in our travels, especially Father and Mother and Colonel Andrews. Dear Lord, may you look over Joe with special attention to his needs and bring peace and reassurance to his family that he will affect a full recovery. For this and all the blessings you bestow upon us each day, we pray, in Jesus name. Amen."

A chorus of "Amens" followed. The servants leave for the kitchen and the only sound for several minutes is the clinking of silver on porcelain.

Johnny breaks the silence, "Grandpa Eddie, are we 'lowd to talk?" Lottie snickers, and Margie muffles a laugh into her napkin.

Edward laughs boldly, "Clearly I am not accustomed to sitting here." He looks at me, "though I think it is quite natural for me." To Johnny now, "I do not think the dinner conversation should be in any way altered because it is I occupying this seat. So, speak as you would otherwise for I have no special news or entertainment to provide."

Margie turns to Johnny and reminds him, "He is not your grandpa, Johnny. Edward is our big brother."

"Grandpa Eddie is our brudder?!" he says excitedly, as if celebrating a great discovery.

Soon there is a cacophony of voices.

Edward has placed me at the foot of the table. It feels like an awesome responsibility, and one for which I have no prior experience, though it provides a grand view of the gathering. Looking around the table, Liz sits to her brother's right. Lottie is in a high chair next to her under her watchful eye. Laura sits on the other side of Lottie. Mary sits to Edward's left; Johnny and Margie next to her. Someone was missing.

"Where is Aunt Margaret?" I blurt out.

"Oh no, my first day at the head of the table and I've misplaced Aunt Margaret!" Edward delivers his confession with exaggerated remorse.

"Is she lost?" asks Johnny, suddenly worried. Margie is nearly beside herself with laughter, looking at Edward, then Johnny, then me, before Liz came to my rescue with a response.

"No," she reassures Johnny. "She went to call on Mrs. Winthrop, just down the road." She points in the direction of Mr. Winthrop's house.

"Oh, you! Wicked nonsense," I say to Edward in mock anger.

Then, sincerely, he explains, "Aunt Margaret is looking in on Mrs. Winthrop this week while she is lying in with her new baby. She is probably helping feed the rest of that family right now. She'll be back before dusk, in time for supper." Edward's smile spreads slowly to fill his face, seeming pleased with his impromptu performance. I easily imagine him as a father with a brood of little ones or a schoolmaster teasing his students mercilessly, but cleverly.

Afternoon naps accomplished and household tasks managed, the evening falls upon us as quickly as the morning had disappeared. That evening Aunt Margaret occupies herself assisting Liz with preparations for returning to school. Edward lights the oil lamp and selects a book of poetry to read to me. Longfellow. We sit close to the lamp so both of us can look at the pages as he reads. He presses his leg against my skirt and I can feel the heat through every petticoat. His voice is deep and soothing.

We are alone and have an opportunity to speak face-to-face about Edward's departure from Harvard and his time in Warren; about Joe and what it is like being here together. I am bursting inside with so much joy that the tragedy befalling my brother seems like a distant memory.

We were the last to retire with no comments about candles from Aunt Margaret. She was long ago to bed. Edward leads us up the stairs with the oil lamp, walking me to Liz's room where she is already slumbering. He sets the lamp on the table by her door and I think he is preparing to light a candle for me to take into the room, but instead, he reaches for me. Placing his hands on my cheeks, he tilts my face up to his and slowly places his mouth on mine. His lips are soft and warm and I am filled with fire and joy. My heart races, heat surges through me, my head begins to spin and fear I will swoon. Oh patience! I want to hide in shame and tilt my head down save Edward see me like this. I lean forward into his chest as he wraps his arms around my waist holding me tight and close. I can hear his heart beat. We stand as still as the night for the longest time. Then, Edward whispers.

"Lizzie, will you accompany me to the Taylors next celebration?"

I nod and then reply, "Oh, yes! Happily."

That day is yet a year away but I would have given that reply to almost anything he asked at that moment. Thankfully, my cousin is a gentleman and I trust him not to request anything inappropriate of me.

"Then it is settled. It will be our secret." He held his finger to my lips.

"Well, goodnight then, my sweet Edward."

"I wish you the sweetest of dreams, Lizzie."

30 August 1851

I have just returned home from three weeks in Methuen and am so grateful that Father allowed me time away from our own home, which has become very quiet since Joe's departure.

While I was in Methuen, I marveled at how Edward took full charge of all the affairs of the house. He managed the servants and saw to it that Maree and Beth were well occupied. He kept track of the comings and goings of all the children. He gave me much comfort, which was especially appreciated now while I have been upset by my brother's circumstance. I will always remember that vacation at the Tenney's. The house was filled with activity and Edward showed great kindness to young and old. The family's daily routine was comforting, though I teased Edward about being too content with his orderly household. He worried I would find him a bore, but I told him resolutely, "You cannot be bored, unless you are boring."

CHAPTER 10

Cross and Sleepy

The Tenney family was one of three prominent families in Methuen during the industrial revolution. The population of Methuen in 1850 was 2,538 residents, compared to Salem's population at that time of 20,264.

Miss M. Lizzie Andrews
Care of Col. J. Andrew
Salem
Massachusetts

Cambridge, [Tuesday] Sept. 2d 1851

My dear cousin,

I am in a horrid condition for writing a letter today, and you must find an excuse for my poor epistle in the fact that I have been unwell ever since I left home and now my complaint has reached its crisis, which causes me to feel very much as any one else who has an abominable headache &c. viz cross and sleepy.

In truth I am hardly able to move from my chair, although I do attend every recitation. "How absurd" then, you will say, to attempt writing in such a condition! True, Lizzie, it does seem very absurd, and doubtless you will find it so ere you finish; but I promised to write to you once at least, before I came to Salem and if I delay longer I shall fail to redeem my promise.

JW will pass the next Sabbath at home with his sister Carrie, and I shall accompany him, thus making my visit to Salem, nearly a month earlier than I anticipated when you were in Methuen. Carrie will pass through Boston this evening on her way home and I should accept Joe's invitation to go into town and meet her if I felt well enough to do so. But I must forego the pleasure and rest satisfied with seeing her on the Sabbath.

We shall probably leave Boston during the forenoon of Saturday in the present week and return to Cambridge very early on Monday morning, after our short visit. Before that time, I intend to call on Dr. Bell and make inquiries in regard to Joe, and I will communicate the result to you when we meet again, if I find an opportunity.

I saw your father in Boston on Wednesday last and he thought it unwise for me to visit the Asylum before at least one week should have passed. I shall probably walk over there on Thursday or Friday if it is pleasant.

I was called away by the car-bell so suddenly on Wednesday that I had hardly time to say "Good bye" and run off. To Laura and Mary I could only nod farewell as I hastened through the yard although they waved their kerchiefs to me as I rode by in the cars. I thought I might meet Liz in Lawrence, but neither she nor Father were visible and I was compelled to hurry on to Boston. - Oh! had you seen the confusion of my room when I reached the College buildings and beheld the delightful manner in which books and boots and dirt were mingled promiscuously together, you surely would have cried "How absurd to dream of living here amidst such a medley!"

But a few days sufficed for placing everything in its proper place, and now although our quarters are not quite equal to a lady's drawing room, yet I should be perfectly willing to receive any of my male friends at any time they might choose to come (after breakfast of course). I am very much pleased with our rooms and I trust that "Chum and I" shall find no difficulty in keeping up our good feelings and mutual harmony throughout the year. - I found very little difficulty in re-entering College; my examination was perfectly satisfactory in every branch, and the only bar to my admission was the fact that I had permitted myself to be drawn in a barouche by four horses, at the request of my class, when I was dismissed in November last. But that matter was finally overlooked and I was entered as a Junior in Harvard College, where I trust I shall remain the ensuing two years without again exposing myself to the disgrace I have once suffered.

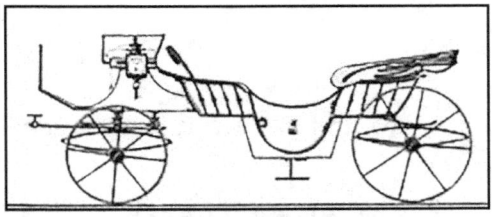

Barouche

Since this sheet was commenced, I have met Daniel Upton of Salem who probably came to Cambridge to witness the great annual game of foot-ball, which has taken place this evening to the discomfiture of the lower classes as usual; in the melee, my foot was severely injured and one eye was changed from blue to black. I believe you prefer the latter color; under the circumstances, I should have wished my "organ of vision" to retain its original shade. But twill all pass away before tomorrow and no marks will remain to show that any of *my* blows were justifiable. These foot ball games are once in each year turned into rather rough sport and whoever ventures to share in them must look well to his safety.

I have written this letter so much larger than usual that I have not room to say one half that I wished. I am sorry that my visit to Salem was so much earlier than I expected; because I think your school has not yet commenced, and you may not find it convenient to be in Salem on Saturday next. If you can leave Hamilton for the afternoon and I can discover your whereabouts I shall be sure to intrude myself into your society; so beware if you do not wish to see your country cousin; for he is a terrible "bore" sometimes.

If I do not have a chat with you, don't forget to write me as soon as you can.

I shall probably reach Salem about noon; so my chum says.

Fare-well for a short time only.

Your aff. cousin
Edward

I have not yet heard from home, tho I shall expect my valise on Wednesday.

Pardon me for daring to write first, but I was compelled to do so, to fulfill my promise.

Daguerreotype of General Joseph Andrews

3 September 1851

Father was part of a military review yesterday in which he was elected Brigadier General of the 4th Brigade of the Salem Light Infantry. There was no barouche for Father, though I dare say he is more suitably a dignitary than my dear cousin, whose only fame is his ribald antics. Still, how handsome and regal Edward must have looked atop the elevated seats.

Senator Tenney and Aunt Augusta attended Father's review. All sorts of dignitaries were casting attention on Father, yet he remained quite unflustered by it all. I cannot explain what all the fuss was about but the preparations were terribly exciting. Father had allowed me to order a new dress to be made in time for the occasion.

Aunt Margaret and Aunt Augusta accompanied me to select ribbons, lace and yardage for the dress, which would be fashioned in the newest style—a very full skirt with brocade trim at the hemline. Father had obtained another large shipment of silk from China and said he would let me select yardage enough for two dresses. I will have one made now and the other after winter. Perhaps my second dress will have an entirely new form in the spring and I will wear it to the next class-day with Edward. No matter how the style may change, I desire for the skirt to completely reach the floor, as I would not dare expose even so much as my high top boots to anyone on the street. My aunts tell me a young lady has been seen on the streets in Salem with a dress that revealed the lace hem of her bloomers. Imagine that! And, she did not seem to mind one iota the attention to her costume or the fact that she attracted every eye of every passerby!

Favoring prudence, my aunts will discourage me from using as much yardage as I intend, but I truly desire the fullest, prettiest skirt I can manage. Aunt Eliza warned her friends at tea last week about a tragedy in which a lady in Boston was killed because of the excessive yardage of her dress! The woman stepped from a carriage and, as she put one foot upon the ground, an abrupt noise startled the horse severely and he pulled the carriage out from under her. She tumbled to the ground, but her skirt caught on the step of the carriage and she was dragged behind it through the town. Oh, it is such a horrid wretched sight to imagine. A terrible tragedy, I agree, but I do not think it is the fault of her dress!

Neither Edward nor Joe was able to attend. Edward had gone off to Cambridge already and Joe, well, Joe remained at Somerville.

--------———⊰⊱———--------

This morning, I joined Aunt Augusta to travel by train to Somerville and bring some cheer to Joe.

When we arrived we were escorted into a large room that was completely undecorated. It was dreadfully cold and completely plain. The walls were as gray as the day outside and the windows were so small one could not see out from them unless at a distance of two feet or less.

I do not see how anyone could feel well there. We waited much too long for the doctor. When he arrived, we were informed that Joe was not well enough to receive us as visitors. The doctor assured us he would let Joe know we had called on him.

Since I had prepared two Sponge-Cakes for the celebration in honor of Father's promotion to General, I kept a piece aside to bring to my brother in a basket with some lemon cake that Aunt Augusta made. It did not fare well on the trip, but we were able to leave it for Joe. I was comforted to think he would enjoy every crumb.

When we left, I was quiet, glad to have made the attempt of a visit, but filled with sorrow for the condition of his new abode. There was not a book or cushion about to create comfort or stimulate his mind. Aunt Augusta surprised me with a question.

"Shall we pay a visit to Edward at Harvard?"

My heart raced, "Oh, yes. Let us do so!"

When Edward answered our knock at his door, he was shocked to see us. His eyes seemed to pop out of his head. I remarked to Aunt Augusta when I followed her into his room, "Until now, this day has been so cold and dark and dreary."

Hearing only the end of my remark, he greeted me with an admonition.

"My best greeting to you as well, Lizzie," Edward replied. Giving us both a peck on the cheek, he continued, "It is a fine vocation to articulate the problems with conditions about which we can affect no change. However absurd it might be to start an enterprise to discover the causes of weather, perhaps it deserves a jolly good try. Would you care to join me as my protégé?"

Edward suggested a brisk walk around the campus and proceeded to march us right out into the chill—I feared merely to make a point about the weather. He was briefly merciless in teasing me about my vocal complaints over something no one can change—the weather. It was all in good fun and Aunt Augusta seemed amused and he kindly proceeded to share his excitement about Harvard. He showed us the architecture describing it in detail and told us his school's history, which began as the first college in the colonies in 1636.

"Imagine the Puritans flocking to classes in those dreadful primitive conditions," I spoke to Aunt Augusta so as to avoid further mocking.

She, turning to Edward, asked, "Do you know how the college came to be named?" He continued, "It was named after Reverend John Harvard, 'tho I must admit my knowledge of him is limited. I think he donated the initial contents of the library."

"It must be very much changed from those early days." I said, musing about what it must have been like to rely so entirely upon oneself and family for all the provisions which we now can acquire through shopkeepers. "It is a wonder the colonists had time for scholarly pursuits at all."

"Edward, you make a splendid tour guide. Thank you." Aunt Augusta was always kind to Edward. "Guiding guests to tour the campus would be a better vocation for you than trying to change the weather."

By the time we reached the station I countered my initial declaration about the weather, with an announcement, "Boston seems somehow brighter, just now, the day clearer than when we began in Somerville."

"Perhaps you have changed the weather, after all," Aunt Augusta remarked.

Edward only laughed. At the station, Aunt Augusta left him with her kisses, which Edward returned.

He proceeded to bid me a similar farewell, with Aunt Augusta watching. Oh, my heart raced remembering his last kiss, 'tho now he merely planted a kiss on each cheek. It was hard to keep my mouth from turning up at the corners as we boarded the platform to take a seat on the cars, which fortunately had to be done immediately.

McLean Asylum 1845

The melancholy I began to feel after visiting MacLean Asylum in Somerville lifted at Cambridge, but the contrast between the asylum and Harvard made the visit with Edward more lovely and refreshing. The weather was dark and dreary but I anticipated the brightness of Edward's warm smile. My face felt as warm as a summer day and the sensation left me nearly gasping. Fearing this revealed my excitement, I tipped my chin away from Aunt August and stilled my breath as I engaged her in conversation.

"Aunt Augusta, does not the daylight in Boston seem to hold more fresh air than that in Somerville?"

"Perhaps it does for you, Lizzie." She responded kindly. After a few silent moments, she added, "Your brother in Somerville is a very different person from your cousin in Cambridge. Their paths are likely to lead them toward vastly diverse destinies." She paused as we watched the trees outside fly by the train window.

"Your path, Lizzie, may be entirely different from either of theirs. Life truly is a mystery. Your correct route through it will unfold naturally in its own time."

"I am going to study hard, Aunt Augusta," I replied, and instantly wished I had a course of study that would teach me to silence my declarations of absurd observations. Why do I speak so freely about matters of little consequence, and hold my notable observations in silence?

———⌘———

With delight, I anticipate a prolonged visit with Edward in two days. The pleasant circumstance of his imminent journey makes a long wait unnecessary. The Sabbath will be delightful to spend with my cousin. Perhaps Edward and I will find time alone and he will take my hand in his, assuming we are free from my sweet pest of a sister. Oh, dread, how she manages to make my romantic notions her business!

———⌘———

22 September 1851

Father is preparing for the annual camp out he is to command of the Fourth Brigade of the Massachusetts Volunteer Militia. The weather is dreadful, however and Father says he might send the troops indoors overnight if it continues in this manner. Emily Oliver says her brother Samuel will also be present in command of the Lawrence Light Infantry.

CHAPTER 11

Back at Harvard

Although it may appear to be common knowledge in the 1850s that a cold could be *caught*, germ theory had not been proven by the medical profession and was not widely accepted. People were as likely to think a cold was transmitted by a chilly wind in a drafty room.

Miss M. E. Andrews
Care of Gen. J. Andrews
Salem, Masstts.

Cambridge [Friday] September 26th 1851

My dear Lizzie,

I hope that a letter from this "old barn of a building," as you most irreverently did style this time-honored Massachusetts hall, will not be less acceptable to you, than would the same epistle be if written in a building of more imposing exterior. If, however, you are averse to receiving a sheet of paper from "the barn," and will inform me of your scruples, I will write my next letter in the library Building (which you thought so admirable for a dancing hall) and then surely if you object, it must be the author and not his room that is at fault. You will see by the engraving above that my room is not in such a dreadful looking building as you think. I will mark it with a X that you may distinguish it. That is Gore Hall (the Library) whose top you can only see, in the background. My room is not visible, being situated on the other side of Mass. but you can imagine me there, employed just now very agreeably. My chum is away, so that I can talk with you without fear of interruption.

I hope that you reached Boston in safety, on Monday after your call at Cambridge, in spite of the cold and dreary weather; for that day was really very uncomfortable, unless one kept within doors. I wish that I had accompanied you to the city, as I might have done, with very little difficulty and without omitting any College duties; but Mother seemed to object, and I could have spent but a few moments with you before you returned to Salem. I shall accept your invitation in my next vacation if I possibly can, and I do not doubt that.

I must thank you again and again for your Monday's visit which gratified me the more because it was so unexpected. I heard some female voices in my entry, and presently a rap at my door, without the slightest suspicion of who was waiting for me to open. Pardon me if I say I thought at first it might be my Goody, though she always enters when I say "Come in." "Perhaps it may be Mother," I thought as I rose to open the door, after the second knock, but that you were with her I surely did not imagine. I need not repeat that I was delighted to see you. The only objection I can find to your visit is that you left too soon; I had hardly time to bid you welcome, before I had to say farewell. I trust I may see you in Cambridge again, certainly, when I graduate, if not before.

Very probably you caught cold on Monday; if so, you must not say that you took it from me, for mine has been rapidly increasing for a week. It became so bad, and caused a headache so severe, that on Thursday I gave up my recitations for a few days, and consulted a Physician, who may half kill me provided I am free from this horrid cold. This has prevented my going to Somerville this week as I desired to, before I wrote to you.

I presume you will hear Mlle. Parodi at Salem in a week or two and of course, you will be delighted with her singing. Oh Lizzie you must be sure to visit Boston when the Castle Garden opera troupe are here, which will be during this winter. I will write you when they come, if you wish me to, and I shall in return, expect to see you in Boston. Then Catherine Hayes will be here too and I hope you will be enabled to listen to her also. She is now in New York and is causing as much excitement as did Jenny Lind. Mrs. Mowat has been drawing crowded houses at the Howard Athenaeum for some time and is to be followed by Edwin Forrest on Thursday next. Some of the Harvard students are perfectly infatuated by Mrs. Mowatt's acting. The worst instance that I know of this folly is that of two Sophomores, who have been to the Theatre every night this term (except three), have always thrown bouquets, and who were so enraptured last night, that they serenaded her between one and two o'clock with a band for which they paid between twenty five and fifty dollars. I have not seen her and do not intend to. I may hear Forrest, though it is possible he will be hissed from the stage, when he makes his appearance; he has rendered himself very odious to many Bostonians by his conduct towards Macready and to his own wife. But this is no news to you, and uninteresting, possibly more so than anything else I may write.

How did your military review pass off? I have heard that Father and Mother were there, and even Mary, notwithstanding my predictions to the contrary. Did Mary say anything about her last visit to Salem or was she inclined to keep silent on that point? I always make her tell me the whole story, when I go home, which she does very readily. I wrote her a long letter today, but I forgot to inquire about the visit before this one.

This term I am studying Spanish and German, which with my French of last year and Italian of next, would make me a tolerable linguist, if I knew anything about either of the languages; but we devote so little time to each one, that a student at Cambridge can only become acquainted with a foreign language by very hard study, beyond what is required by the college faculty. For our Spanish instructor we have a man between seventy and eighty years of age, and from such a teacher it is not to be expected that we can learn very much. The German is quite difficult, but the Spanish is very easy. Shall you study either of them at present? If so, I wish you a better Spanish teacher than I have, but a better German one you can not find.

Have you attended Mr. Frothingham's church since I was in Salem? I am confident that your time was spent in listening attentively to the sermon and not in vainly endeavoring to satisfy yourself that a stranger's hand had left its mark upon your fan, as you so boldly asserted was the fact. If you have discovered anything it is chargeable to a cousin of yours, who lives in Salem, and is rather fleshy; this same cousin I have heard, had his hats severely bruised by a young lady "once on a time." Perhaps you have heard of the same occurrence?

Now I have succeeded in spoiling a clean sheet of paper, notwithstanding the combination out of doors to prevent me: for "the day is cold & dark & dreary" and all Nature seems to have determined that I should not write today; but she has not succeeded in preventing my saying something, though I can not answer for anything beyond that. I shall expect to hear from you soon and perhaps I may meet you in Boston, ere long. That depends upon yourself, however; because I shall not fail to find you if I only know when you will be in town. Excuse me for writing in so small a hand today, but I forgot your desire till I had covered half a page and then I thought it too late to make the change. I hope that you will be able to read this, notwithstanding. I shall delay sending this till Monday, that no one may say I wrote too soon after seeing you. I have not heard from home for some time, but I hope Liz has not been so neglectful to you as to me.

Good bye - - - - I am ever your affectionate cousin Edward.

Saturday evening - As I seal this letter, I can not refrain from filling up what little room remains, even at the expense of tiring you to death. I have been to see Charlie Pierson today, and learned from his chum, (Santos) what fine times you have had in Salem this week with Military and Horticultural shows and displays. Of course you did not attend school all this week. I shall not go to church tomorrow on account of my cold which is hardly any better than it was. My chum is in Boston, I expect, as I have not seen him since morning. The weather is no pleasanter than was yesterday and I wish I had another letter to write to you. I have no doubt you will despair of ever reaching the end of this document and wish that your cousin would not write such horrid long letters. But never think that I wish the same, and never fear to tire me by writing too much. I have been reading in Longfellow's poems today: I admire them very much; you must not fail to read them if you have time, particularly his ballads and miscellaneous poems. Parodi has a concert tonight in Boston and one tomorrow. I should long to hear her, but for my cold, I don't know when she will go to Salem. Mother and Mary have returned to Methuen before this time I presume. Do you know when Caddy Osgood is to be married? I should think you would freeze if you still stay at Hamilton. I hope it is not quite so cold there as here, however. Have you seen Joe Brown lately? He was in Salem a few Sabbaths since, I believe.

I do not expect to return home till Thanksgiving unless some accident should call me from Cambridge. I can't find any more room (for which you are very thankful?) and must say farewell, and close my letter for fear I may be tempted to add more tomorrow.

"Good bye, Lizzie,"
Do you remember!

Gore Hall, Harvard University Library

The dreadful weather continued. The chill settled in my blood and I began to suffer a sore throat, wishing for some licorice tea with cayenne. Oh, that Edward's Goody could have been available to care for me as she does so well for him when he is away from his own mother.

It seemed I stayed in bed for days on end, listening to chimes of the tall clock hour after hour - wondering when might I regain my strength and feel better – the next hour, the next day? I have never been so ill. My throat burned and I could barely swallow, my neck felt thick and stiff. The heat from my head and behind my eyes would prompt me to throw off my quilt and coverlet. Within minutes, shaking from chills penetrating my very bones, I climbed to the foot of my bed, full of self-pity, to retrieve the dear cast-aways and bury myself alive in them. Aunt Eliza came to my room nearly every hour to check on me, bringing me a most wretched tea brewed of wormwood, sage and marigolds boiled with crab claws. After days of worry, she came with something different; it was a smile on her face.

"Your cousin Edward is here. He knows you are not well and has no desire to disturb you but has brought you a book to read. Are you well enough to receive him?"

"Oh yes! I would be pleased to see him if I may have a few moments to dress. I will meet him in the parlor." I do not know how I found the strength. I feared Aunt Eliza would hurry me back to my room once she saw me, for I covered my sleeping gown with only a housecoat and a warm woolen shawl. Pulling my hair into a knot at the back of my head, I buttoned on my shoes and headed down the stairs. Half way down, my head felt light and I had to stop and brace myself. I sat on the bench at the landing, feeling stars spin in my head as Edward's image emerged bit by bit with the tap of his shoes on the wooden stairs. I was ready to stand and continue my journey when he reached me and placed his hand on my shoulder to guide me back to the bench. I was so stunned I could not resist for I had never been touched so tenderly by a man before, except my father and barely that. His touch sent a shiver the full length of my spine. I sat.

"You look pale, Lizzie." Edward reached down and put his open palm against my forehead. He seemed to hold it there for the longest time. I was beginning to feel so much better. In fact, I was feeling quite warm under his touch.

"You feel warm."

"Oh, no, I am fine now." The hall clock ticked its steady pulse and the desire surging through me was building with each tick. Be still my heart, lest the clock's impending chimes send me full into his lap.

"Should you return to your room and lie down?" he seemed worried.

"Lie down?" In your arms, please. My wicked thoughts did nothing to cool my temperament and in my nervousness, my mouth began to emit word after word, though their meaning was inconsequential to my true feelings.

"I have not had much activity in so many days. I fear I have nearly forgotten how to walk. My limbs are soft and barely recall how to move from one place to another." I knew it was a sign of poor breeding to speak so plainly of my own limbs and to a man at that, but this was my cousin, and I could not seem to help myself, so I granted myself forgiveness! A rush of warmth returned to my head bringing crimson to my neck. I wanted to bury my face in my shawl.

"I have brought you something, Lizzie." Edward said.

"Yes, Aunt Eliza told me." He handed me a book. My eyes fell upon it resting on my lap. The book was bound in the most exquisite brown leather. I opened the cover slowly, feeling my hands tremble, as he watched me closely to see my response.

"This book is the writings of Sir Walter Scott. Have you read his work? Do you feel well enough to read?"

"Oh yes, thank you. I have not read this whole time I have been unwell, but am eager to do so. I am feeling better by the minute."

Edward laughed and a smile filled his face. I turned my eyes and felt that flush rise again to the top of my head. I did not say another word as Edward sat beside me on the bench and continued cordially.

"I have read many of his works and find his cadence compels me to read on. 'Tis as if the reader is carried forward on the rhythm of the words and the story can only unfold at one pace no matter who is reading."

"Hmmm," was all I could say.

"Well, I did not intend to tire you, so perhaps I will bid you farewell now. I do hope you feel better, Lizzie." He leaned slowly toward my cheek and brushed it with a warm kiss as he rose and turned away from me.

"Edward." He stopped. "Thank you. Truly. Thank you…" I paused.

He looked at me as if there was more to say.

"For the book. Thank you for the book. I am sure I will enjoy it."

"It is my pleasure. Rest well, Lizzie," he said, and his back filled my view.

I watched as he moved down the stairs, his foot tapping each step, his torso rising slightly before dropping to the beat of each foot landing. At the bottom, he turned and glanced back, nodding with a slight smile. My smile was in no way slight. My feelings spoke to me as if in a foreign language I could not interpret. What are these feelings? Does he feel as I do? Surely he must know how I feel and feel it too.

———— ⤬ ————

Father's promotion is a month past and the activities do not seem to cease. We have been entertaining at home every week's end. Not a one seems to be tired from the activities, however. More than a dozen persons are gathering to celebrate Father. The dining room is full. Father holds the center of the conversation, though he is mostly listening. The men surrounding him are lighting cigars and sipping cordials.

I move into the parlor with a cup of tea and hear a deep voice say, "Who is your friend, Laura?" Mary giggles, and one can barely hear Laura's response. Behind them, Aunt Augusta and Aunt Margaret sit in the sunroom gazing out the window at Aunt Eliza's garden in back. My aunts have great enthusiasm for flowers and some have sustained their blooms, even as the temperature is cooling off at night. She is modest about the mastery of the garden, but very willing to share the view with them.

"She is not merely my *friend*, Leverett, she is my *cousin*, Mary Tenney." Laura speaks up. I stand in the archway between the dining room and parlor, catching conversations of the men behind me, and the ladies in the sunroom to the side. In front of me, Laura's naturally soft voice rises over the din of the nearby conversations.

A tall and stately young man stands in the exact center of the parlor, "It is nice to meet you, Mary. From where are you visiting?"

He is the only gentleman in the room, and this is the only room with a mixed crowd. There are so many young ladies on Chestnut Street, he is a welcome sight. His hair is dark and shiny, parted cleanly down the middle and he wears sideburns that handsomely reach the line of his jaw. He rests one hand on his hip, his waistcoat pulled back to reveal his slim build. I try not to notice. He reminds me so of Edward!

"I hail from a country township north of here, from Methuen," Mary replied. "Mary, this is Leverett Saltonstall." Laura completes the introduction.

"It is truly my pleasure to meet *you*, Mr. Saltonstall." Mary's voice lilts and she bats her eyes when she speaks. "How do you come to be attending on this occasion?"

"You need not address me by my surname, Mary. Please call me Leverett." I understood Mary's formality, for Leverett was a lawyer and twelve years older.

The help seem to glide as if on ice skates between the parlor, dining and sunrooms to freshen drinks and offer cakes and cookies, then slip back to the kitchen.

"Leverett lives down the street." Laura informs Mary, although not strongly enough to break Mary's gaze from the gentleman's commanding figure.

I step toward Laura to join their conversation, when Margie motions me to sit next to her on the fainting couch. As I pass Laura I hear Leverett explain, "Yes, my family has been friends with the Andrews since we moved here. Colonel - I mean, General Andrews, has been so kind as to welcome us into his home on many occasions." Leverett sees me pass and adds, "Lizzie has done as much as any to bring the neighbors together in each other's company." Mary hangs on his every word. How could he *not* continue to talk?

"Our fathers have also had business with each other."

"What does your father do, Leverett?" Mary asks.

"He passed away six years ago."

"Oh, my. I am so sorry. I have heard the name Saltonstall mentioned so many times in family conversations, I did not know he passed."

Lowering her eyes, she continues, "My mother died soon after I was born." Laura sees that I am watching, but remains expressionless.

Leverett returns the inquiry, "My sympathy to you also, Mary, that you have never known your mother."

"Thank you. That is so kind of you. Perhaps it would have been more difficult had I known her."

"What does *your* father do, Mary?"

"He is a Senator, for the State of Massachusetts," she nearly spells it out to emphasize the impact of her father's position.

"It seems both our families are in politics! My father was, at one time, the President of the Senate." Leverett nearly bows as he nods his head toward Mary. Very charming, Leverett, I thought. Laura has become invisible to them both. She does not seem to impose her presence by speaking.

"Your father must be a very able and intelligent man," Mary says.

I am enjoying their conversation when it is interrupted, or rather when Leverett becomes distracted, for Rose Lee has entered the parlor and is approaching him.

"Good afternoon, Rose," Leverett beams, even brighter than he has with Mary. "Let me introduce you to Lizzie's cousin from Methuen."

Why, Laura has become completely invisible, indeed, and now Mary is fading fast in Rose's presence.

"Nice to meet you, Mary. Hello, Laura." Rose offers courteously before she turns to Leverett to await his next move.

"Would you ladies please excuse me, I mean us, for a moment?" Leverett asks.

Mary stands motionless, and Laura comes alive to respond, "Of course."

As Mary and Laura swish past me, I hear Mary lament, "Oh Laura, was I much too forward? Will he think me a complete fool?"

"Oh, pooh," Laura responds, and tries to ease Mary's concerns. "Leverett and Rose are always together. Since childhood. There is nothing you said that could make that any different." Laura continues to reassure her cousin as they disappear into the sunroom.

---

11 October 1851

Edward's recent letter has filled me with news of the latest entertainments in Boston, and even New York. It must be exciting to be so near grand singing entertainers. 'Tho it is frightful what becomes of people under the influence of these great performers. Society becomes completely swept up in the excitement of their appearances. It is completely absurd. 'Tis no wonder Edward thinks I wish to shield myself from hearing one more bit about the feud between Macready and Forrest. However, though it is more than two years past, it is still prominent in many people's awareness. Though I was just 14, I was little aware at the time and now do wish to know of such occurrences, not to indulge myself, of course, but to be informed.

Edward and I read an article of the account this past summer as more news continues to be revealed about Mr. Forrest. The news has by now spread throughout Boston and one's views on the subject have become a seemingly necessary topic of conversation. The sad events have split our very society over the value of such entertainments, some flocking to hear more performances and others, like myself, fearing to go near. I recall it was not long after it occurred I overheard a conversation in my own home.

When Reverend Thompson first came to warn Father, I sat in the parlor, a short distance away, reading a book and heard everything.

Rev. Thompson's voice boomed, with true exasperation for the embarrassing behavior of his fellow man. "Joseph, I experienced firsthand the circumstance between Misters Macready and Forrest. The situation left me shaken but grateful I had not been injured or worse in the melee. The audience groaned and hissed. Some were yelling, 'Off, off!' while others cheered, 'Go on, go on, go on!' It was total pandemonium. Banners were displayed with 'You have ever proved a liar!' and signs were held above the crowd with 'No apology, it is the truth.'"

I could not believe what I was hearing. This is not a situation about which Rev. Thompson would typically express such impassioned views.

He continued, "Then came the song of the witches..."

Was he still conversing about Macready and Forrest, I wondered. Or could he be speaking of the witch trials?

"...and the crowd began to chant, 'Where's Macready?' I dared to question whether this was truly Macbeth or another witch-hunt of its own making! The uproar continued and increased, completely upstaging the actors, until the performance had to be suspended at the end of the third act, and the audience was directed to disperse."

Father interjected, "The open letter to Macready in the newspaper urged him to continue his performances, but he would have been wise to resign his engagement at that time."

"Who could have known what was to come, were he to continue?" Rev. Thompson asked of no one.

What was to come? I wished so badly to know. I was embarrassingly spellbound.

Rev. Thompson's voice fell to a murmur, "If only he had known." Looking up, he explained his statement, "He was persuaded by the urgency of some of our worthiest and prominent citizens. They deplored the riot, and prayed for him to remain, to give the better class of the community a chance to manifest their approval of him and their detestation of the riotous proceedings."

"He did reappear?" Father inquired.

"Yes, and the situation grew ever more troublesome for while Macready was at the Astor Place Opera House, Forrest posted his intention to play Macbeth at the Broadway Theater the same night! The fans of Forrest issued notices about organized meetings, and published an exceptionally inflammatory card in the *New York Herald*."

"What did the card say?" Father asked the very question I was thinking.

"It urged people to buy tickets and take possession of the Astor Place Opera House on the night of the performance."

"Surely that card warned the authorities to make counter-preparations," Father remarked.

"Oh, yes, and it succeeded. The sale of tickets was refused to persons of suspicious appearance."

"Now, that is a difficult situation," Father mused, "for who can say how one might fairly judge a person as suspicious, and not restrict the very freedoms that our constitution promises?"

"All those offering to enter were carefully scrutinized, but it was not left to one alone to judge the character of those who entered. After the audience had assembled, the doors and windows were closed and barred and three hundred police guarded the house, inside and out. The house was filled with persons of exceptionally high character, in general, but a few of the disaffected had entered. Soon Macready appeared, and was promptly hooted by several persons, who were evidently and purposely located in different parts of the auditorium, in order to give a general character to the manifestation. This was followed by their projecting missiles, thrown directly at him on the stage."

"And you were in the audience that very night?" Father spoke with the same amazement I was feeling. But, of course, Rev. Thompson would have been admitted, being of the highest moral character.

"Yes, I was. I wanted to see a complete performance. My wife did not join me for the repeat performance, and it is a blessing she did not, for you can only imagine the great fear and confusion in the audience, until the police arrested the ringleaders."

"So, there *were* arrests." Father seemed relieved to know someone was trying to maintain order.

"Yes, the police succeeded in restoring confidence, and the performance was permitted to proceed."

"Well, good, then. That is a relief."

"Oh no, it was not to last. A mob of thousands gathered outside and around Astor Place as the performance was underway in the Opera House. That crowd made a general attack upon the police."

Rev. Thompson was speaking more softly now and I moved, quietly, from the fainting couch to the parlor chair by the door. Father's jaw had fallen completely open and he pulled his head back in disbelief, or disgust. I could not tell which, but it signaled Rev. Thompson to continue.

"They overcame the police and endeavored to storm the building by battering in the doors and windows."

"Was that when the Seventh Regiment was called?"

"Yes, they had been held in waiting and it was then that they marched up to occupy Astor Place, preceded by cavalry. The horse troop was averted by an attack from the mob and the horses became unmanageable in the wild scene. Colonel Duryee ordered his men to load with ball. Recorder Tallmadge proclaimed the Riot Act, demanding all to disband immediately. But it was without effect, whereupon Sheriff John Westervelt ordered a volley over the heads of the people."

Rev. Thompson stopped his story, and I held my gasp, so as not to be found out.

With great emotion, he continued, "The shots killed and injured inoffensive men and women. Such an ineffective and cruel manner of proceeding! It is unfortunate, but so common in such cases."

He lamented, "It both angered *and* encouraged the mob, which responded with a fierce attack on the regiment. A well-aimed volley followed, and only then did the mob retreat. Astor Place was restored to order, but it was only temporary, for the mob shortly returned from Third Avenue and attacked with pavingstones!"

Father showed concern and queried, "Did the crowd consist of young men? So often, the young ones are easily rallied to follow a protest, especially if they have been recruited from the taverns. Such stone throwing is the same tactic the Irish immigrants have used to try to turn away the French Canadian immigrants who threatened to take their jobs. Irish confetti, they called it."

I imagine the crowd was indeed filled with young men, thinking of the riotous behavior Edward spoke of at Harvard, and that was by men who are scholars of the highest moral character. Surely these tavern patrons were a different breed.

Rev. Thompson explained, "Well, the stones were hurled alright, but only to be met by a third volley of shot from the muzzles of the police and infantry. That finally scattered them, but at too great a toll. That final firing killed seventeen and wounded twenty six."

As a member of the military, Father was all too familiar with the outcome. "The entire affair wounded one hundred and forty one of the Seventh Regiment and many of the police. In all, thirty four of the mob and innocent spectators were killed, and a great, though unknown, number were left injured."

I could not remain quiet, and emerged from behind the curtained arch, "Whatever became of Macready?"

"Lizzie?" Father exclaimed. "Were you listening?"

"Yes, Father," I admitted. "I could not help myself. I am sorry, but I have already heard much of your conversation, and I must know what happened to Macready."

"Come sit. First I must reprimand you for this behavior, Lizzie. A man has a right to maintain privacy in his own home, and when you find yourself close enough to overhear a conversation, you must dismiss yourself directly and discreetly, or reveal your presence and excuse yourself from the scene. On occasion, you may request permission to partake in the conversation, but what you have done here is improper and rude. Do you understand?"

"Yes, Father," and after a reasonable pause, I had to ask, "Well, may I? May I join your conversation?" I was comfortably seated, and made no motion to leave.

Father looked at Rev. Thompson, "She has already heard the worst of it, I suppose." He nodded to me, and to Rev. Thompson, he merely said, "Please continue."

Somewhat hesitantly, "Macready escaped. Still in costume, he left by a rear door of the Opera House and was secreted for two days in Judge Emmet's house. He was forced to proceed in disguise to Boston, and he sailed from that port for England."

Father wanted me to understand. "Great praise was given to the Seventh Regiment for its self control and gallant conduct under orders."

To my great surprise, Rev. Thompson revealed in my presence, "The next day a meeting of the baser sort was held in the Park, where inflammatory speeches contrary to law and order were made. These, however, led to no action; or at least none more than to spawn the nickname of 'Massacre' Place Opera House. I do not know how such an undesirable sort could have entered past so many police."

Father continued to direct his comments to me, "An investigation of the matter revealed that tickets to the theatre were gratuitously distributed to such persons by some of the parties who signed the card calling upon Macready to fill his engagement."

Now, Rev. Thompson spoke to Father, "Surely, you have heard that Ned Buntline took a conspicuous part in this riot. He was arrested, convicted, and sentenced to one year's imprisonment, with a fine of two hundred and fifty dollars."

"That is not to be a surprise to anyone who knows of his character. He has gained much notoriety as a writer of sensational stories featuring unseemly subjects. It appears he used his talent with words, or misused his talent, to create handbills designed specifically to excite the supporters of Forrest, causing them to be drawn to the scene of the

146

riot."

That was the end of the topic for the night, but Edwin Forrest has remained the subject of public conversation.

When I next saw Edward, he told me Forrest was now in litigation with his wife. Edward explained, "Edwin Forrest was incensed with N. P. Willis on account of that gentleman's action and expressions toward his wife. So, Forrest met Willis in Washington Square and knocked him down. He proceeded to lash him very severely with a flexible cane. Willis cried for help and a crowd gathered and was disposed to respond, but as they approached, Forrest shouted, "Stand back, all of you; this is a family matter!"

"So Willis had violated Forrest's wife?"

"I am not certain there were any violations, except for the shame she brought upon herself."

"I feel for that poor woman! To be married to a beast like that. Perhaps she was simply seeking protection from Willis." I allowed Edward to know the mix of sympathy and disgust I felt and yet was strangely compelled to share with him what I had heard from Father and Rev. Thompson.

"Why would audiences flock to performances by ill-reputed characters, such as Forrest and Macready?" I questioned.

"The tragedy of these performers is absurd." Edward agreed. "The Astor House spectacle truly is a sharp and drastic contrast to the charm of a company like the Castle Garden Troop whose excellence was witnessed by too few. Those scanty audiences enjoyed an idyllic setting. In summer weather, they were surrounded by moonlit water and cooled by the sea breezes. It is an altogether delicious place of amusement, Lizzie, yet perhaps it is shunned as too sentimental."

"Edward, what is to become of our society that neglects to partake in civil performances but flocks to observe and even participate in such senseless violence and the tragic occurrences such as this that result?"

"It seems they do not know they make it worse by their attention to it, Lizzie. Certainly we cannot change what others do. Perhaps it is our duty to enjoy the finest performances when presented the opportunity, and not indulge those that are less worthy. I would like to do that with you, Lizzie. You would be safe with me, I am sure."

"Oh Edward, I would like that. More than you can imagine. I pray that we will share such opportunities." I imagined sitting close to him, so close the warmth of his presence would entertain me as much as anything appearing in front of me on the stage.

III. Preparing for Professional Life

Edward's grandfather was an elected official who shared a political ticket with Samuel Adams and John Hancock, and associated with Paul Revere. At the time Edward was born, only twenty-four states had entered the Union. His father, an attorney, held political positions at the local and state levels in Essex County and Massachusetts State, while his uncle was appointed Consul to Portugal by President Andrew Jackson.

CHAPTER 12

——•———⚯———•——

A Fierce Looking Pedagogue

Miss M. E. Andrews,
Care of Gen. J. Andrews
Salem – Mass.

Cambridge, [Saturday] Nov. 8 – 1851

My dear Lizzie,

Thank you 10,000 times for your last letter! "Too long?" Why that is perfectly absurd: 'tis impossible. I shall *always* have abundance of time and a superfluity of will to read as much as you can write: so never fear on that account. But when *I* write, I become so much interested that I think not of the feelings of anyone but myself, and I still keep on, heaping nonsense upon nonsense, totally regardless of what a mass I ask my friends to read. I hope no one would feel it a duty to read more than was agreeable to them, but there may be exceptions: therefore I must shorten my letters in future. It is not to all, I am anxious to write so much, and doubtless the others are very thankful to be excepted.

Since I received your letter, chere cousine, I have attended a concert of the Quintette club, seen the handsome August, and of course I was delighted with the music. The selection of pieces was said to be inferior to their former concerts yet *I* thought it admirable. I was very agreeably surprised by the whole exercise and especially by the execution of August Fries. Of all the pieces, I was most pleased by a duet from Kummer by the brothers August and Wulf. The club will give a series of concerts in Cambridge, but I regret that absence from college will deprive me of the pleasure of attending. I suppose you have heard the Club in Salem, this season, or you will soon.

Nearly twenty of my classmates and cronies are going to teach school this winter, all of them within a few miles of each other. They wished me to join them and I was desirous to do so, but I needed my father's permission. I persuaded him to give me that, and now nearly all is settled, and I intend to turn country school-master for ten or twelve weeks.

Imagine me, a fierce looking pedagogue, sitting behind a pine desk with all the dignity I can possibly display. "Here, you little rascal, come up here! Why didn't you learn your lesson? Hold out your hand!" Whack! Whack! sounds the ruler. "Now go to your seat and study." Possibly you might also witness fierce struggles between the Master and some "big boy," where the pedagogue often fares poorly, and returns with a black eye, half his dignity fled away. But I don't anticipate much of that sort of exercise; on the contrary, I expect to find much pleasure. I shall keep a full journal of my first experience in this novel life, and if it does not contain some laughable scenes, I shall be disappointed.

Perhaps you remember my saying at Mr. Downing's, I should teach school in Salem. I know you did not believe it, but here is the first stepping-stone to that position, and my words may prove truer than you thought. You promised also to be one of my scholars; don't forget that.

I stood, last evening, for three or four hours in the most oppressive crowd I ever saw. It was at a Whig meeting in Faneuil Hall, which was addressed by Rufus Choate and Judge Thomas. There was no space to move in; I could not turn round or even breathe freely and my body was nearly crushed bones and all. To escape was impossible till the crowd should go, and stay I must, willing or not. Had I been squeezed a little harder, then woe to all my visions of pedagographical (oh! murder) glory! Then many a young idea, now destined to shoot forth most gloriously, would be confined in the groveling mind of some noble youth, because your cousin, "the master," did not direct it. "Pooh! Nonsense!," adds Lizzie when reading this; but I am confident that I shall make a most remarkable instructor.

I have not yet decided where to go, nor am I certain of obtaining a school.

For one reason, I am very sorry to leave college; it will deprive me of the pleasure of seeing you in Boston as I shall not return till March, after the Opera troupe will have left. Then I shall have only two weeks of vacation instead of six; I wished to spend some time in Salem this winter, but I fear it will be almost impossible. Please write to me before Thanksgiving, and I can tell you where I am going and what I can do.- I called at Somerville on Wednesday last, to inquire about Joe. I could not see him, and was sorry that I could not learn that he was better. The Dr. says that he is perfectly contented, but does not seem to improve very rapidly. I have called twice to see him since I last wrote to you. They never allow me to see him, but the physicians are always ready to give me any information they may possess.

I hope you are entirely free from your cold. When do you return to Salem? It must be very cold at Hamilton now. We have had snow here once. I walked from Boston last evening. It was a splendid night, and I could have walked till morning, with pleasant company. If you visit Boston before Thanksgiving, be sure to inform me of your intention.

Good bye ---
Your affectionate cousin,
Edward

---

30 November 1851

Aunt Eliza and I went to Somerville to deliver another package to Joe before Thanksgiving for we knew he would not be at table in Salem for that occasion.

I did desire to deliver my package to Joe; however, I also secretly conspired to make a surprise visit to Edward, 'tho I am certain he would have preferred seeing me with some forewarning. Were it possible for me to please him in this regard, I would oblige his preference; but in this circumstance I feared that our fondness for each other would be revealed if I disclosed my plans to my traveling companion. I could not think of how to suggest such a visit to Aunt Eliza without raising her suspicion, for to provide a letter to Edward of such a plan would require that the arrangements be confirmed well in advance of our trip. I surmised that were I to casually suggest a stop at Harvard College to say hello to cousin Edward, I would appear spontaneous, avoiding any pretense of having a too-great desire. With no hint of suspicion, I would therefore prevent future difficulty for Edward and me in our desire to spend time together in the future. We are simply the closest of cousins.

Never did it occur to me that my casual suggestion to Aunt Eliza would be met with a resounding "No." I was dumbfounded and spoke not a word the whole train ride back to Salem. I was, however, successful in one matter; the only suspicion I affected in Aunt Eliza was that I was somehow not feeling well. In truth, I was luminous with not fever, but anger at my own stupidity for preparing every bit of my scheme in my mind except the very thing that was to face me. Did she think I wanted only to deliver a parcel to my brother?

Father has not yet been allowed to visit Joe in person and it has been more than three months that he has been confined.

Tonight is the first time we have been without Joe at the dinner table on Thanksgiving.

Father was the first to the table, seeming to display a mood that nothing was amiss.

"Come, Lizzie, Laura. Aunt Eliza will be to table promptly. Please be seated so dinner may be served." He looked at us and I saw pain in his smile, standing in sharp contrast to the flat cheeks that Laura and I wore. My sister did not say a word, sweeping past me and plopping herself at the table.

"Laura Josephine, what trouble have you seen now?" Father demanded. I wanted to speak for her, but knew it was best if I were to bite my lips closed.

"No trouble at all, Father." Laura was not convincing. Her eyes rose slowly to make contact, pulling her head toward him so slowly one would think she were a lady three times her age. Father's face froze somewhere between sympathetic and stern, but truly was neither.

"Father, it is not right that Joe cannot be here!" Laura revealed her angst.

Realizing my selfishness, I spoke now, "Father, I feel the same. What is Joe doing this day to celebrate Thanksgiving? What has he to be thankful for and what have we to be thankful for when he is not here?"

"What has he to be thankful for?" Laura echoed, before Father had a moment to respond and continued, "We have never had Thanksgiving without him. Can you do nothing to bring him home?"

"Can you do *some*thing to bring him home?" I could not help but implore. I felt so sure that Father was the only one who could repair the fracture in our family. Surely, he could do something!

Father took a deep breath. "Lizzie, you know Joe is not well, and is not fit to join us."

Aunt Eliza had slipped quietly to the table, "Girls! Where are your manners? Your father is right. I know it is difficult, but please try to understand."

"We do not understand," Laura offered meekly, looking at me for reassurance, "Do we, Lizzie?" No longer feeling so bold, I said nothing but my face said it all as I shook my head.

I could see Laura struggling to keep tears from rolling down her cheeks. Her chin quivered, and her mouth was drawn in tightly to hold back her words. The silence was loud.

Father's voice broke the quiet. "We shall speak more of this later. This is not the time, and the Thanksgiving table is not the place." Father intended to have the last word on the matter. His patience beat like a metronome as he led the Thanksgiving blessing. How could I be so mistrustful of God's plans for my brother? How was I to be sure that I was not to be of more help to Joe in this matter? Those were my inquiries of God.

With strained cheerfulness, Father followed the blessing by beginning a conversation. "We are gathered here to give thanks for all our blessings, girls. We must make a point to remember those things for which we are truly grateful." Then, he inquired directly of me. "Lizzie, for what are you thankful just now?"

"I am thankful that Joe is near Harvard, for he will have cousin Edward to look in on him—once Dr. Bell says he may have visitors."

Laura looked at Aunt Eliza and pleaded, "Will we be sent to an asylum if we misbehave?"

I had already caused too much commotion at the table and I should be an example to Laura, but I was proud of her finding the courage to speak her mind.

Father responded, "Laura, such a thing would never occur. Joe did not go to the asylum because he misbehaved of his own free will. He is not being punished. He needs to be near a good physician to provide his treatment; and Dr. Bell is perhaps the most noteworthy and acclaimed physician of his sort in the country. We are fortunate he practices at the McLean Asylum and that institution is so near."

I wanted to jump from the table and run to my room like a little girl indulging a temperamental tantrum. I wanted the comfort of sobbing in my feather pillow and the freedom to be childish and distraught. I clamped my jaw and stilled my breathing to maintain some degree of composure.

Father looked at Aunt Eliza, with eyes that seemed to say, 'Please help me with these girls, dear sister.' He never uttered a word, but Aunt Eliza seemed to hear the cue.

"Lizzie. Laura. Can you tell me your favorite memory of a Thanksgiving past? Is there one in which you remember Joe being here that is memorable for you?"

"I remember last Thanksgiving. Joe was singing under his breath the whole of the dinner! Do you remember, Laura? He said he was dreaming of Jeannie with the light brown hair."

Laura's eyes brightened. "I do. I remember, he was perfectly giddy."

Father sighed a long drawn-out breath, as if he had been holding it all evening.

Aunt Eliza asked Laura, "Perhaps you would like to prepare something special to bring Joe for Christmas. It would brighten his day. Shall we plan something?"

"Oh yes, let us plan to make him some very special sweets. He enjoys your cakes so much Lizzie. Will you make him a Sponge-Cake?"

"Of course. Perhaps we can each make something and let him decide which he thinks we should prepare again?"

I knew from that moment that there would be no conversation after dinner about doing anything more for Joe. It was clear that he was not fit for society – not as a dinner guest and not even as a topic of conversation. Laura and I needed to show Father that we could behave. We could be respectable, and maintain a cheery disposition, even when we were confused and our hearts were breaking with loss.

---

10 December 1851

Thanksgiving is past and now we look forward to the events of the Christmas holiday. Today we have been to the Lees to arrange riding to the Quintette concert in Salem next week. We will go in Father's sleigh together. Father surprised Laura and me with tickets as he knows how eager we are to hear August Fries perform.

The concert was mesmerizing. As the final curtain fell Laura and I stood to join the audience's ovation. Then we remained briefly and I whispered my confession to her, "August Fries is so handsome I could barely divert my eyes from staring at his very presence. He must have seen me. Do you think he did?" Laura just smiled and snickered, "Perhaps."

"Do you like August the best, Lizzie?" Laura interrupted my daydream.

"Oh, yes. He is so striking in his appearance, and the manner in which he creates his violin to sing is unlike any I have heard. Yes, I find him most enchanting."

"Then I will like his brother!" Laura announced. "Perhaps one day we can meet them and invite them to tea, Lizzie."

"Oh that would be extraordinary, would it not, Laura?" She and Rose giggled and I continued, "Do you really think he can see us in the audience when he is on stage?" I asked in earnest.

"Perhaps he can. I am certain he could see your fan, Lizzie. Perhaps you could make a mark upon it that would distinguish it from all others."

I feigned a glimpse in my bag as if to find my fan. "My fan! Oh, Laura, I have left my fan upon my seat. I must go back and see if it remains there."

"I will make haste, but if I am detained, you take a ride now. I will find a ride back with Rose's sister. I saw she remains here still." I left the crowded foyer and walked back through the doors into the theatre

157

making my way down the aisle to the front. An usher approached me.

"Are you lost, young lady?"

"No, sir. I left my fan on my chair. May I retrieve it?"

"Let me assist you."

"Oh, that will not be necessary. I know just where it is."

"Please allow me," he insisted and began down the aisle. "Where were you seated?"

Of course, we would find nothing there for I merely wanted another glimpse, but August was nowhere to be found. Neither was my fan, for as only I knew it was in my bag the entire time. But I had to save face, so played along.

"In the front. The very front." I followed him past the rows looking fervently for any sign of August.

"I am so sorry, Miss. Your fan does not seem to be here. Perhaps it has been found and returned to the front and is now awaiting your inquiry. Shall I see to that?"

"You are so kind." We ventured back to the foyer, only to find that no one had found my fan – to my great surprise and dismay, which I acted out accordingly!

Emily Oliver watched me emerge from the theater and gestured for me to come her way.

"Would you like to join me in my sleigh? I would enjoy your company," she said.

After excusing myself from joining Laura and the Lees, I rode home with Emily feeling enlivened by the evening's performance. We shared stories of our families and brothers, including her older brother, Samuel, whom I have seen at military reviews. He and I have not yet met. I shared a bit about my own brother. A striking contrast! Her brother sounds like a consummate gentleman, so bright, strong and gallant. She said I must meet him some time. (I hope to spare her a meeting with my own brother!) I might think hers as handsome as August. She insists he is. She insists it must be so if it is said by a sister! We discovered we knew many people in common and left each other with feelings of great affection and promises to continue our conversation when we meet again at another occasion.

CHAPTER 13

Home on Vacation

Miss M. E. Andrews
Care of J. Andrews Esq
Salem
Mass.

Methuen, [Monday] January 26 1852

Dear Lizzie,

I have undertaken to write to you twice since I received your last letter, but you know I am at home and it is almost impossible to exist ten minutes without interruption. I can never write letters in vacation although I have nothing in particular to occupy me. If I attempt to write at Father's office, he continually interrupts me to do something for him; I must obey, of course. If I sit down at home, I have hardly time to get ink and paper in readiness, when Johnny, Margie or some of the children break in upon me with their chatter. I usually dismiss everyone from the room till Lottie comes, and I can't send her out, so I have to put up my pen, and play with her instead of writing to you.

Were you ever told that Lottie resembled you? It is so and - but I won't say more or you will charge me with flattery.

My good fortune detained me in Cambridge a few days after our term closed, so that I received your last welcome letter in good season. Of course, I shall come to Salem, if it is possible, as soon as I can, but I expect to remain at Methuen until near the close of my vacation.

On Friday (the week before last) I attended the Musical Fund Rehearsal in Boston and saw some girls (mille pardons! - ladies -) from Salem, the Whittredges, Daniel Upton was with them. I never saw them before but Peirson pointed them out to me from the gallery. I saw "August" too, of course, and I mentioned to him your anxious inquiries for his welfare! Oh! What a fib! I shan't sleep well tonight. I would scratch it out, but twill spoil the looks of my sheet. So please pardon me the first(?) fib I ever told.

Emily Oliver called to see Liz on Monday with a Mr. Briggs, a young lawyer of Lawrence. Liz says that E. is engaged to him, but I don't believe it. Emily told me that she saw you in Salem, but she did not say that you "had to wait for the sleigh" after the Quintette concert. I give you credit, Lizzie, for an excellent invention. I presume you left your fan at home that evening - and for that reason you had to wait for the sleigh. I am determined to disguise myself as August Fries and go to Salem some evening. I warn you to look sharp at the last concert (I am too late for the 7th tonight) and see if you can detect me. No doubt your sleigh will call for you late if you tell Edward beforehand.

I wish you could hear Anna Thillon sing. She is at the Howard Athenaeum, and sang at the Mus. Fund last Saturday.

Have you seen JW this vacation? When you meet him, ask him (not from me) how he will spend his time, and perhaps he may invite you to share his sport. I expected to visit him, before I return to college, but he is alone in his house and I am puzzling

162

my brains for some other expedient.

On Thursday, before I came home from college, I called at Somerville and saw Dr. Bell. He said that Joe seemed neither much better nor worse than he was, and that his health was quite good. I have not been able to see Joe yet and the Dr. says that none of his friends have been permitted to.

I saw in the Register a notice of Edwin Carlton's death, at sea. Poor fellow, he had hardly been gone from home a half year.

Do write to me soon, dear cousin, before my vacation closes, and tell me when *you* have a vacation.

All are well, excepting troublesome colds. I hope you are free from the prevailing coughs &c. I wish you some happy, pleasant sleighrides.

Ever your affectionate cousin

-"Good bye" - Edward -

---

31 January 1852

Aunt Eliza's voice was so soft it barely roused me from my slumber. "Lizzie, are you awake?"

"Hmm. Ah. Yes. I am waking. Is it morning so soon?"

"No. It is not yet night, Lizzie. You have barely closed your eyes. You took to bed right after dinner."

"Hmm."

"Lizzie, I know you have not felt well all week, but you have a visitor. He appears to be rather anxious to see you. Shall I ask him to wait until morning?"

"Wait until morning?" I felt the cloudiness falling away from my thoughts. Did she say 'he'? "Why, heavens no, Aunt Eliza, I shan't sleep the whole night thinking he is at the stair awaiting my appearance tomorrow."

Aunt Eliza corrected my lazy form of speech, "You mean you *shall not.*" Then she laughed, "He is staying the night, Lizzie."

How is that amusing? I wondered, still foggy with sleep.

"Who is here, Aunt Eliza?"

"It is your cousin Edward."

"It is *he* who will stay here tonight?" That is a different story completely. I did not allow Aunt Eliza to see my true excitement, but calmly replied, "Why, yes, I would enjoy his company."

"Well." She hesitated. "Do you plan to receive him at your bedside, so you may continue to rest?" She reached for my robe, which hung carelessly on one of the tall posts at the foot of my bed.

"Here? In my housecoat? Heavens, no. I shall join him in the parlor, if you please." My feet slid into my slippers made by my own hand, and I remembered they were much like the ones I had fashioned for Edward. He has seen me in my robe and slippers before. I stood as Aunt Eliza helped me into the robe, which she covered deftly with a long shawl. I glanced in the looking glass as my aunt disappeared out the door.

How dare I present myself to Edward in this state? I pulled my loose hair tightly into a knot at the nape of my neck. My head still spinning from standing so quickly; my heart raced as I began walking down the stairs. I grasped the thick mahogany banister tightly with each step as I heard my aunt advising Edward to meet me in the parlor. Edward stood, unmoving, his face turned to me as I descended.

"Hello, dear cousin," he beamed.

"Hello, Edward."

"Did you catch another cold in the sleigh after the concert with August Fries?"

"It seems so." I stopped and leaned against the wall to steady myself, placing my hands behind me against the mural on the wallpaper.

"Lizzie, you look as drawn as that pastoral scene behind you."

"Oh, my. Please excuse me, Edward. I am not as fit as I had hoped. Is Aunt Eliza nearby?"

"Yes. I am here," she said, as she rounded the corner and looked up the stairs toward me. "Lizzie, you are pale as a ghost. Perhaps you should return to bed. You will have time to visit tomorrow."

"Oh, no. I will be fine once I reach the fainting couch in the parlor."

"Edward, will you please assist her?" Aunt Eliza beseeched him.

"Of course." Edward bounded gingerly up the steps to my side placing his hand behind me, he barely touched my clothes, yet I could feel the warmth from his hand. Then, he wrapped his free hand around my arm and pulled me toward him to provide support, urging me to lean toward his frame.

As he placed me on the fainting couch, he asked, "Shall I find you a quilt?"

"No, that is not necessary, but perhaps you can cover me with that knitted blanket," I said, gesturing to the corner, trying not to point, for he was not my servant, and I did not want to be rude. I did, however, wish to settle my head into a pillow on the arm of the couch. He leaned over me and spread the blanket covering my slippers, which he seemed to notice were similar to his own.

"Thank you, Edward. I am sorry to subject you to such a sight. I must look completely frightful. I have been confined to my bed the entire week and I think I will die."

His eyes opened wide, jaw slacked, as if he would speak.

"You do not look like someone risen from one's deathbed, Lizzie. In fact, you look rather extraordinary, I must say. Like a delicate flower." A smile spread across his face. I tried not to show the effect his endearing comments provided, though I could not hide my pleasure.

"It is boredom that is likely to be the death of me, not any other cause."

"Well then, I have just the tonic for that!" He pulled a carved wooden armchair closer to me and settled into it. The sun was setting outside the window. Edward reached over and lit the candle on the table nestled against the thick arm of the couch. He looked toward me and I instinctively turned to see what he might be viewing. The light flickered across the scrollwork at the top of the couch. I had known

165

this furniture all my life. When I was small I would pull myself onto the couch and trace the scrolls with my fingers. I turned back to face Edward and realized he had been looking at me, not the scrollwork.

"Is that the cure for my ailment? A candle?" I redirected his gaze to the subject of my comment.

He turned to me again, "I have determined that your case is serious and will require much more than that! You need a good dose of poetry to drive the evil from your blood."

"Please promise not to send me running from my room with recitations of the death of Marmion," I begged.

Edward laughed. "Your wish is my command." He picked up the tattered copy of Charles Dickens' *David Copperfield* from the table near the candle. "I will read you Dickens if that is the tonic you require, m'lady."

"Oh, Edward, it is so kind of you to come. I would treasure anything you care to read or say, and that is not only for relief from my boredom. I may even impose on you to read me your last letter, if you would be so kind."

Edward was suddenly speechless, 'tho he recovered instantly. "My letter? You have it?"

"Yes, but do not fear. I destroyed the note you enclosed in it. Although now I wish I had not, for that is a sentiment I long to hear spoken from your very own lips."

"Lizzie." He looked at me, leaning his face close to mine. He lowered his voice and continued. "I think I remember every word I wrote on that sheet." He closed his eyes, and began.

"If one were to light passion in another
Who drank the fire into his soul,
Both would be filled,
Not emptied, by the transfer,
Rather together made whole.
If one were to cool the fever in another
And take the heat into his heart,

166

Both would be made well,
Not harmed, by the transfer,
Secured to never drift apart."

Edward's voice lingered in the room and we remained silent for a long time. His verse had truly begun to restore my health. My throat felt suddenly cool and still. As the murmur of conversation fell away in the distance, Edward reached over and laid his hand softly on my arm.

"Oh, that you would let me take away anything that causes you harm, my pet, and we could live in each other's hearts forever. That is what I hope for us, Lizzie," he whispered.

I closed my eyes and let his words fill me. The darkness under my lids made his touch warmer and all the more comforting.

"I hope for that, too." I whispered in return. Without opening my eyes to see if he had heard, I let my head rest heavily against the small brocade pillow that adorned the arm of the couch. The tall clock at the bottom of the stairs ticked out the heartbeat of the house, in perfect rhythm with my own. The warmth of Edward's hand remained, as he lifted it from my arm to pick up his letter. His words moved smoothly from his serenade of sweet talk to an almost scholarly description of Capt. Thomas Cook Whitridge, his wife Susan Louisa and their three daughters. He slowly recited their ages, as if he were checking his files, "23, 19 and 17, I believe."

He then began to reminisce about Charlie Pierson who he described as, "the son of my father's doctor."

Next was Emily Oliver. Was this gossip? I wondered, though I did not care for I longed to hear his impressions of my friend Emily. Edward would not be convinced by anyone that Emily was to be engaged to Mr. Briggs. Neither of us could have known then how Emily's life would one day entwine with mine.

Now came Edwin Carlton's death at sea. "My cousin!" Edward exclaimed. I stirred to open my eyes and, seeing him, felt so deeply his loss. He explained, "The notice of his death was in the Christian Register and I am certain was widely read as he was the son of Oliver

Carlton, who is most certainly the most prominent teacher we have known at Salem's Latin School." He paused only briefly before offering a fine distraction.

"Dickens," he said, "Shall I read to you?" Leafing through *David Copperfield*, Edward began reciting the page marked with a silk ribbon. It was David Copperfield's description of his devoted nurse and advisor Clara Pegotty. After David's mother dies, Pegotty is discharged. Edward read as if he knew she would later marry but be reunited with David after her husband dies. He read:

"'She laid aside her work (which was a stocking of her own), and opening her arms wide, took my curly head within them, and gave it a good squeeze. I know it was a good squeeze, because, being very plump, whenever she made any little exertion after she was dressed, some of the buttons on the back of her gown flew off. And I recollect two bursting to the opposite side of the parlour, while she was hugging me." I was lulled to sleep by Dickens, or was it Edward's soothing voice?

When I awoke I was in my own bed. I opened my eyes to see the sun break through the curtains, and rest upon my face. I vaguely remembered how Father let Edward carry me up the stairs last night. I forgot, in that moment, that I had been ill.

By morning, I was feeling quite spry. I nearly begged my cousin to stay another day, but he had commitments to honor. So, with feelings of admiration, mixed with regret, I bade him good-bye. I now await the long letter he has promised to send and I to do the same.

———✺———

14 Feb 1852

Aunt Laur has given birth to a baby boy. He has been named Frank George Allen. Little Mamie is delighted to have a brother!

———✺———

Daguerreotype of Mary Elizabeth Andrews circa 1853

22 Feb 1852

Uncle Joseph E. Stearns Sprague died yesterday. Poor Aunt Sarah and JW, losing his father in his last year of school, and so suddenly to the curse of apoplexy. At least God graced him with a final joy of meeting his only grandson. Our whole family participated in the funeral procession to Harmony Grove Cemetery and watched sadly as his coffin was lowered into the grave. His published will stated "my last request to such of my children who shall survive me is that they will not differ with each other in the division of the little property I may have, but that either may sooner be willing to give up his own share rather than take any advantage of each other; that they may all live in the cultivation of love and harmony amongst themselves; that they may be useful members of society and blessings to their race, and thus insure that happiness and peace of mind which no wealth can bestow." Rev. Frothingham presided.

CHAPTER 14

The Opera

Music has always seemed to play an important role in each new generation's tastes and identity. It was no different in the 1850s, except that the popular music of the time was opera.

Miss M. Lizzie Andrews
Care of Gen. J. Andrews
Salem
Masstts.

Cambridge, [Thursday] March 4th 1852

Dear Lizzie,

Only think: I could have remained ten minutes longer than I did on Monday last, and then have reached the cars in full season. It was dreadful provoking, I assure you, to be told that I had nearly a quarter of an hour wait in the depot, when I had, but one moment before, counted each second an hour. But all mourning for the past was useless and I found no *great* difficulty in keeping sane till the train arrived. Then too, as I skulked by

Mrs. Sprague's house, I felt conscious of committing a fault in not calling there before I left Salem. I saw some of the family at the window, but I ran across the street as if I were in a great hurry and feared to miss the cars. As I rode home, I thought over my abrupt departure and I felt that I had done very wrong in leaving as I did. I hope my friends will attribute my neglect to youthful folly and ignorance of propriety to be expected from one bred in the country, and not suppose that I had forgotten them in their affliction.

I trust, dear cousin, that you were able to go out on Tuesday and I hope by this time you are as well as ever and much happier for so tedious and unpleasant a confinement. I am glad that I was not persuaded to remain that "one day longer" in Salem, as I had to leave home on Wednesday noon and I was occupied with Father's writing till within an hour of my departure. I dressed myself, made everything ready, packed my trunk, bade all good-bye and ate my dinner in less than an hour and this time too I had to wait the cars arrival in the Methuen depot. As soon as I reached Boston, I made my purchases (not very extensive ones,) paid some bills due, bought a ticket for the Opera, rode to Somerville, called at the asylum and saw Dr. Booth, nearly froze to death in walking from there to Cambridge because there were no cars, built my fire, found a monstrous great Valentine in the Post office, took tea and rode to Boston just in season to obtain a good seat. I'll mention that valentine again.

The opera was the Puritans and I was glad that you had not selected Wednesday as your night for coming to Boston. I suppose all your friends will say it was beautiful &c. but I know you would have been disappointed. The opera is a very fine one indeed, but I thought it was poorly cast. *I* was very much disappointed. Coletti, the bass, sang miserably; the tenor only tolerably. Bosio was very pleasing, but not nearly as good as I anticipated. Badiali, the baritone was admirable. I have heard him before and last evening he sang better than all the rest. Of course it was a treat to go, but if I had but one night to choose, I certainly should not select the opera of "I Puritani" as represented by this troupe. Coletti, at any time, is a poor singer and last night he had a cold, was sick &c. and yet he had a very prominent part to sing. I am certain that Maretzek has far the better company, for I have heard the leading singers that are now with him; yet I would not advise you to wait for Maretzek, as it is uncertain if he will come to Boston, but come before this troupe leaves and if Maretzek comes, come then also by all means. (Corporal) Lee was there and Mr. Gillis, but I am unacquainted with both. I saw no Salem ladies present and I looked in vain around the house for "l'incognita." "La Favorite" is announced for tomorrow, but I shall not attend. I may go to the Mus. Fund Rehearsal in the afternoon.

As I called at the Cambridge post office, the Postmaster handed me a great, square envelope, that reminded me at once of your black plaster, only much larger, which I supposed was a valentine. Thank fortune 'twas prepaid, so I carried it to my room, opened it and found a beautiful sheet, with bouquet &c. and a long page of writing - from whom do you think? It was mailed [postmarked] "New York" and signed "Aunt Fannie," but its authorship was very evident. It was from the lovely Miss Sedgwick, who sought by this means to win back her long-lost, wandering love, Poor girl! I'm afraid she'll not succeed this time; yet it is too bad that all her pains-taking should be for naught, so I shall tear off the writing and send the picture to "Pegotty." She gives me plenty of good advice and hopes that I "may pass the portals of college life unscathed." *Somebody* said "I hope so too," once on a time - (and on a different subject) which *somebody else* will always remember with gratitude. Pray burn this letter, for 'tis too bad to laugh at poor, sick, sweet, sentimental Miss Sedgwick and there is a bare possibility some one besides yourself may see it. But I am obliged to postpone the rest of my letter for a short time and I wish you good-bye for the present. It is late at night and I hope you are sleeping soundly and enjoying the pleasantest of pleasant dreams.

Good bye –

Friday afternoon 5th - You see I am not at the Musical Fund Rehearsal as expected. I obtained a ticket this morning but I am expecting Father to see me today and I am unwilling to run the risk of his calling in my absence.

I have very good news to tell you from Joe. When I called on Wednesday afternoon there were several others in the room to converse with Dr. Booth and I detained him but a few moments, long enough to hear that he was improving and that I could write to him as soon as I chose. Accordingly I wrote four pages to Joe yesterday and sent it to Dr. Bell before beginning your letter. I told him of home, all I knew of "the Josephine," and whatever else I thought would interest him, but I made not the least mention of course, to his present position nor why I had not written to him lately. If I receive an answer from him, as I expect to, I hope our correspondence will be kept up for a long while. I did not press my desire to see him as Dr. Bell said the Supt. would prefer to have none of their patients visited by their friends unless at the request of Dr. Bell. Dr. Booth remarked that if Joe's father should insist upon seeing his son now Dr. Bell would probably consent, but he should *prefer* not to have him (i.e. Uncle J do it. Under these circumstances it would have been improper for me to go farther than express a desire to see my cousin, and I told Dr. of my intention to write to him soon.

Our studies this term will be harder than they have been, but still I shall have plenty of leisure to read all those *long* letters you have promised to write to me. I shall watch the mail daily for one and will have a friend ready to assist me in carrying it to my room if it should prove too long and heavy for me to carry alone.

174

You see I was in earnest about writing and I have written you today about as long a letter as I well can on a single sheet. But don't say that I am complaining, for I prefer to write long letters to you, if you are willing to receive them and to reciprocate.

When are you to hear the Mendelssohn Quintette in Salem? I wish you in anticipation a pleasant evening and a delightful chat with August in the ante-room.

Liz Tenney says that Emily Oliver has had the same sort of a sore throat, which she caught at the same time and in the same sleigh with you.

Father has just been here and has left me a supply of money, so that I am as happy as when you came down stairs last Friday noon. I wish I had four pages more to write to you and even now I am strongly tempted to burn this up for the sake of re-writing it again. Remember now, a very long letter will be expected very soon and I will answer it as soon as I dare. "Good bye!"

Still later - Pardon me, chere cousine, for practicing my old trick of disfiguring my sheet in this way, but I can't see my letter lying here without continually adding by little & little. I shall keep this in my desk till Monday morning or you'll think I am writing you "soon" with a vengeance. Tomorrow afternoon & evening there will be four musical entertainments - one operatic concert & a rehearsal in the afternoon & two concerts in the evening. I shall try to go to Boston some time during the day. I wish you could be here too. The Germania rehearsal in the afternoon will be admirable. I did not intend to write here for fear you can not find a beginning or an end to these sentences. Be sure & send a good long letter, as soon as you can.

Your affectionate coz -
Edward.
Good bye till I hear again from you -

Sat. night - "Oh dear," You say, "will he never end?" I have just reached my room from the Germania concert & can't omit telling you something about it. As you may have seen by the papers there was an unusual performance, consisting of Shakespeare's "Midsummer night's dream" with Mendelssohn's music. I never saw the melodeon so crowded before. -Even the stage was covered with spectators, only reserving room for the company. The overture to this piece is the most magnificent thing of the kind I ever heard. The "Wedding march," which Caddie Huntington played last Sunday was performed very finely. Miss Kimberly sustained the reading of the play; but although she is very pretty, her reading is not of the highest order. Perhaps you may remember, when I was in Salem some time ago, we heard Fanny Kemble read this play, without Mendelssohn's music.

Dear Cousin, I might have added another page & saved all this scrawling here but then 'twould seem much longer and I should not attempt it till I saw how you received long letters. If you write me a long one I shall judge you like them.

I see that there is no announcement as yet in the Salem papers of the Quintette concert, but I hope you can hear them soon. I have not succeeded in obtaining that introduction to August, I promised to. If I do I'll give him a note for you as an excuse for calling. How will that do? Here is just room left for me to bid you good night and repeat the same wish as of last night. Be sure to write me very soon.

Good bye -
brother E - (the Quakers say brother)

11 March 1852

Oh, conscience! Why did *I* not send Edward a Valentine? Dare I reveal something that heretofore is known only by him and me, and my dear diary? He does not need a card to know he is my valentine, and on this occasion, Cupid must see we are destined to marry.

There, I have admitted what before was only in my deepest thoughts, and it must return to that depth until the time is right for it to be otherwise. For that matter, even Edward must not know too soon the depth of my feelings for him. It would be entirely inappropriate for me to be too encouraging, for he must only believe—never be certain— of my feelings for him. I would not be so brazen as to expose my tender sentiments prematurely, lest I become the next Miss Sedgwick.

I went about my day considering whether I might be the cause of poor Miss Sedgwick's loss of affection from Edward. If it is so, I have no regrets. It is meant to be, unless I am a fool, or worse, a temptress, to think that I may have stolen his heart from her. Perhaps, her attractions grew as he achieved a degree of notoriety after his dismissal from Harvard. Certainly she was sympathetic, rather than deterred in any manner by that mishap. Surely, his intentions must have been to be kind to her, nothing more, and she mistook that for some other affection. In this day, sympathy and sentimentality are not qualities that bind someone like Edward to another. Quite the contrary, I trust he prefers a lady who does more than swoon after him. It can be most difficult keeping on one's feet when in his presence, or for that matter when reading his charming wit laid 'cross a sheet of paper. Edward's wit and decisiveness do attract one.

Father, too, has such wit and decisiveness, but my brother has only wit, it seems. Oh, my poor brother, I fear he has only half a wit, indeed! I cannot bear to think of Joe in that horrid situation, locked up like an animal, not free to come and go, yet I cannot easily sweep those thoughts from my mind. What is his crime? Is he a danger to someone—to anyone—for not conforming to society's expectations?

Father is having a shipmaker in Maine build him a vessel for his import business. It is called *The Josephine*, a name which bears no relevance to its purpose, unless, as Edward may be wise to see, this is Joe's ticket out of Somerville. He could surely find a way to work on the ship.

Oh, how I wish Father would demand an audience with his only son. Edward would have done as much were Joe his. Of course, I am at a total loss to affect any change is this situation. Still, mustn't I try *something* lest he grows ancient and forlorn for lack of contact from his family?

——————❦——————

2 April 1852

I am filled with anticipation and hopefulness for my dear brother. Dr. Bell says Father may bring Joe to Boston to purchase paper and ink for Joe's drawing. A leave from the asylum could contribute finely to his progress, and I think Father welcomes the direction as to how he might guide him. I feel a greater fondness for my father since Joe was removed from our home ten months ago. Perhaps I should not have experienced his removal with so much peace and joy but, truth be told, I felt relieved he was in the care of someone who could understand him and his needs, for I certainly could not!

Father arranged for Joe's short leave as part of our preparing for travel to New York. We will remain there for five weeks. I am to help Father receive a shipment of silks and to help record the inventory of goods. Since I am almost seventeen, Father can trust me to keep a watchful eye on each bolt that is offloaded and indeed I do have a keen memory for recalling various colors and patterns. The work will keep my attention, for now as the train clanks along the rail, I can think what I wish, and, of course, thinking of my cousin is my greatest pleasure in life.

Father also has some banking business to attend to but we are making it a holiday together. I am certain I will not see Joe until after our return, but feel assured he will be well occupied during our absence. I will not see Edward either, though I have given him my address so

Dr. Luther Bell

we may continue our correspondence. We will reside at the Pollard's. Kate Pollard has written me of all the fine attractions to see during my visit—grand architecture, theatrical entertainments and shops. She has also warned me of the pigs that run wild in the streets of New York. Although they do a splendid job of keeping the garbage off the streets, of late they are known to also keep people themselves from venturing from the sidewalks. Children and small ladies have been knocked to the ground when too many large pigs run together. How absurd!

Kate intends to take me to shop for charms that I may bring back to Laura and Aunt Eliza. I may not have the courage to see the sights, if the pigs are running wild!

Father is to meet several ships that will be arriving from China. He said I may accompany him, and assist him in selecting silks for ladies dresses. What a glorious occupation for me!

---

16 April 1852

I am in New York with Father and Kate. What a thrill to be here in time to pass my seventeenth birthday in just three days. Kate and I have become the best of confidants as a result of all the time we are spending together promenading through New York, most often just the two of us.

The sun was high in the sky by the time Kate and I left her home to begin our daily walk. The sounds of the ships pulling into the Harbor brought me faint memories of Salem. I say faint because it was only enough to remind me that the ocean smelt the same; what filled my nose was completely different. Instead of one salty smell, half a dozen indistinguishable scents mingled, among them garbage, pigs, and the sweat of workers. We walked on and at the next corner the air was filled with the finest spices. Vendors lined up in rows and called us as we passed.

"Ladies, buy the finest oregano and rosemary from me. Two shilling. Half pence. I take any money. You like this. You not go away with nothing for your family. This is the best spices in the world."

"Imagine that!" I remarked to Kate. I felt it rude not to respond, but Kate clasped my elbow and redirected my attention. She said nothing, only moving me along—so many times that I began to understand how differently I must behave in a city of this magnitude.

I could not help but compare New York with Salem or Boston, for I have been away three weeks already. The air was thicker. The same sky was somehow not as blue. This one was filled with a mix of the familiar—horses trotting and panting, laughter and conversation—and the unusual. Languages I could not understand rose up from the din of the crowded streets.

I raised my voice to be heard above the crowd, "Kate, may we stop at the post office to see if I have a letter?"

"Why, yes, of course, Lizzie. It is not far from here. Did you not receive a letter from your sister already this week?"

"Yes, I have. And one from Aunt Eliza last week. I am hoping to hear from my cousin."

Kate laughed. "Lizzie, you have so many cousins, there is a good likelihood you will hear from one. Is there one in particular you have asked to write you here?"

"Well, yes, but I would be happy to hear from any, of course."

Kate did not inquire further...until we reached the post office.

"Have you a letter for Miss Lizzie Andrews? It would be in care of Miss Kate Pollard."

"I believe I do. Let me check, Miss Pollard." The postmaster disappeared into the back room.

He emerged with a smile. "Just as I thought. One came in two days ago. I was wondering how many more I might receive before you two ladies returned. This one is quite thick. Seems to be a good long story here." He handed the letter directly to me. I felt the heat rise up my neck and I wanted to turn away before it rose to my cheeks.

"Thank you, sir." I turned to leave, hoping Kate had no other business there. Glancing at the letter, I saw it was from Edward and tucked it in my bag. Kate was right behind me.

"Is that the one you expected?" she asked.

"Yes. The very one," I said softly. I thought I heard Kate utter a softer "hmm."

"Shall we stop at the Astor House and rest our feet? That would give you a chance to read your story, I mean your letter," she teased me. "You were looking a bit shy at the Post Office, Lizzie. Seems you have a special letter there."

She was not so rude as to ask me directly for information about my personal affairs, but I could tell she would not rest easy until I gave her some explanation.

"A rest would be welcomed," I replied.

We entered the lobby of the Astor House and found a comfortable sofa. Kate ordered us tea. I opened my letter and began to read. I had always read my letters from Edward in private, and now I sat in the middle of the afternoon, in a busy city, with direct company and no one seemed to pay me any mind. Kate was watching the people walk along the wooden sidewalk. As I turned to page two, I peeked behind me to be sure no one was reading over my shoulder. A woman in the finest silks and furs passed us. Kate nudged me, "Did you see that? Her attire must have cost her two hundred dollars!" I could not take my eyes off her. She was exquisite and so very elegant.

The very next moment, a woman shuffled by, close to the buildings, wearing nothing but rags. Honest to goodness rags that the ragman would buy for no more than a shilling. The two women promenaded the same street at the same time! "Imagine that!" I uttered before I realized I had done so aloud.

Kate took that as an invitation for a conversation.

"Have you news from home?"

It took me a long time to know what to say.

"Oh, Lizzie, I am not asking you to read me your letter, but I am so very curious what in it has got your tongue."

"It is a letter from my cousin Edward."

"Edward?" she paused. I did not reply. "Edward Tenney? Is he not your brother's age?"

"Yes."

"Do I see that the letter is from Cambridge? Oh, Lizzie, you must tell me about him."

I explained that we had been writing since his first year at Harvard in a casual manner, as cousins, but in fact, had grown rather fond of each other. I told her more about him than I had ever told anyone, leaving out the most private of our discussions and of course never mentioning his dismissal from Harvard and subsequent time in Warren.

"Is he not the son of your Aunt Augusta's husband and not really a blood cousin then?"

I nodded and she continued, "Oh, Lizzie. He sounds just like a character in a book I am now reading. You must read it. I will buy you a copy today."

She paid for our tea and nearly pulled me to my feet before I had time to finish Edward's letter. Through the rest of the day I wondered what I would read on the final page.

The sights of New York were no comparison to New England. There was not one book shop but many. Kate quickly found the book she was seeking, *The Wide, Wide World*.

"Reading this will occupy you later, but you must let me show you where they are building one of the *finest* hotels in the wide, wide world," she laughed as she emphasized the last words, sounding like a vendor seeking to sell me a piece of New York.

Hotels were everywhere, and just as she predicted, two stood out to me as exceptional – the Astor House Hotel where I had read Edward's letter, or at least began to read it, and the new Metropolitan Hotel, just now being built. Kate told me the Metropolitan would be completed in August and suggested I ask Father to bring me there earlier in the day when crowds gathered to watch the construction and tour the site.

Having ended our day with a mere glimpse of the Metropolitan Hotel, the next morning I did ask Father if we might take a tour of the site and he was delighted to fulfill my request. We stopped there on our way to view the silks and toured the site, which consisted mainly of standing afar from several angles and hearing complete descriptions of what is to come.

These evenings have been among the happiest I have felt. I have been thrilled to visit so intimately with both my dear friend Kate and my dear father. They are two with whom I can share thoughts of my dear cousin.

---

23 April 1852

I sat after supper with Kate to finish reading my letter from Edward, to write to Joe, and begin reading the new book she had given me, *The Wide, Wide World*. I must confess I allowed her to read my last letter from Edward. I know I should be ashamed as he has begged that I not share a one, but I was weakened by its beauty and could no longer contain my feelings within myself. I have been entirely discreet at keeping our romance private from all the family. Kate knows what would be fitting and proper and I simply had to confide my secret with someone! It gave me a sense of comfort to know I could share as much with her and she would keep my confidence.

---

1 May 1852

Dear Joe,

I hope you are faring well and have chance to feel the spring weather at Somerville. As you know, Father and I are in New York. Today I helped him select and record descriptions of some very fine silks that he has purchased from China. This is the most exquisite selection I have ever seen anywhere. I selected a dark blue silk to have a shirt made for you and will find other colors for dresses for Laura and myself, but I do not want to bore you with that.

I thought of you all day, wishing you could have seen the building site for the Metropolitan Hotel. Allow me to describe it for you, so you may enjoy a visit to New York, even if only in your mind's eye.

The hotel will be six stories high! It will have five hundred rooms, some with immersion baths in the very rooms! In a most delicate manner, the tour guide described that one of the floors is intended to allow the guest to attend to those everyday matters for which most of us rely on a chamber pot. Excuse my departure into such sordid details, Joe, but I believe I have had a remarkable glimpse into the future and want you to imagine it, as well.

We were not able to view the frescoes on the walls inside the suites but they are intended to be splendid throughout. That is something that we will need to make a point to see some day, my dear brother.

The furniture is to be perfectly suited to the room, with mirrors in abundance. The lobby, adorned with tapestry carpets, will be filled with rosewood sofas, lounges and chairs. We were able to view the location of the dining room and I have never seen so wide a room completely unsupported by columns. Windows will open onto Prince Street on one side and a courtyard garden on the other. The ceilings in most of the rooms will be elevated and the windows will create an illusion of spectacular vastness.

There will be pipes that bring gas into the lamps continuously, so they can burn for long periods of time without needing to be tended for refilling. I have seen as much in Salem, and now Father is talking of fitting our home to be equipped in this manner.

I heard about steam boilers that will pump cold and hot water into each room. Have you ever heard of such a thing before? The pipes for the hot steam cause every room to be heated while the windows open to allow fresh air and ventilation. Oh, the comfort of waking to a warm room without needing to have a fire built and tended. I learned so many things I had never known possible.

Perhaps this is nothing new to you, for you are so clever when it comes to designs for buildings. I hope you have a chance to see this some day.

I hope to see you instanter.

I remain, ever your sister,
Lizzie

---

12 May 1852

I have been occupied with writing letters during my stay in New York and now that I have returned home I am reflecting on the city's vastness. It had an overwhelming magnitude that I could not have imagined had I not seen it for myself. 'Tho 'tis but twelve miles in length and no more than two miles across before the city reaches one of the rivers that confines it. Within that area it bursts with streets and markets and people everywhere at all times, and the smells to prove it. Trains and ships move to and fro, the way children run to their mothers when in need, only to break away when they have had enough.

The city gives life in much the same manner as a great mother, and it can exhaust one the way a demanding child can, for it seems to never rest. One must tear one's self away and say, 'No more!' with great discipline to get a moment's peace.

We walked along Wall Street, the very place where the great businesses of the world are born.

One entire afternoon was devoured at the Astor Library, a magnificent building made of hewn granite. It was a gift from Mr. Astor to the entire public at no charge for admission. Kate P. tells me Mr. Astor was barred from access to a library as a youth, so when his determination and good fortune made him a wealthy man, he never forgot the importance of a city having public access libraries.

We visited the Crystal Palace and it was every bit as magnificent as I imagined, though they say some of the most valuable items have been removed. When there are so many free sites to visit, this one has a difficult time by comparison and cannot strongly justify a fee.

The Astor Hotel and the Metropolitan Hotel were beyond compare and I am determined to return to see the latter in its grandeur upon its completion, dreaming that my return may be at a time in which I may accompany Edward to that very Hotel—though not in any inappropriate way, of course.

Other hotels, such as the Claredon, the Collamore and the Irving, would be beyond grand in Salem, but in New York they sit dwarfed by the two great giants and the utter vastness of the city.

Kate and I promenaded daily in public, without an escort or a worry about walking alone. We viewed as much as possible, though we kept as brisk a pace as was befitting two ladies. The churches we saw were beyond description in their elegance. I did wonder, however, where the many poor people I saw on the streets went for worship. Certainly they did not have the attire that would permit them entrance to such elaborate cathedrals.

The contrasts in attire I observed were unlike anything one would see in Salem. Now Salem seems ever so quiet and still compared to the excitement of the streets of New York. I will miss the sight of so much fashionable society. Why, even the carriages were adorned in a manner I have not seen in Salem—with tapestries decorating the outside of the doors with the most lovely pastoral scenes.

Though, with all of this, I was most stirred by the vast beauty of the Hudson River. We crossed High Bridge and enjoyed such natural scenery as is becoming rare along the streets of New York. The forests and groves were thick and lovely. It looked like Paradise and I wished Edward could have observed it with me, though I imagined—in a most shocking vision—just how Eve fell to sin, being lulled by the peacefulness and comfort of such indescribable beauty.

Still, by the fourth week, I longed for the familiar. I wanted to smell the salt from the sea as it wafts onshore, laying a coat of white on the rock walls that line the Harbor; to feel the breeze that refreshes me on a warm summer day and hear it rustle through the leaves on the trees as I venture down Chestnut Street toward the Train Depot. I wanted to gaze out the window at James with his nose to Bobby's, speaking in low tones as he pats him and readies our carriage in the morning.

How I missed sitting around the dinner table in my own home with Aunt Eliza, Laura and Father hearing Margo clanking spoons against cooking pots in the kitchen, her Irish brogue a melodic undertone to the meal.

Father and I have barely arrived home and tomorrow we leave again—this time all of us to see Joe. Finally, my brother will be free to leave and dine with family—at first, not at home, but with the Fellows in Chelsea. He is not to have too much activity or diverse company, only family. Edward will join us, however, as he is anxious to see Joe, and to see me, I hope, although that is not what he revealed to Father regarding his plans to join us. He will come from Cambridge for the afternoon, and then Father and Edward are to return Joe to Somerville.

I hope Edward will slip me another note to carry home, since our time together will be short and so very public with all the family. Or, perhaps he will continue his Spanish expressions, and only I will understand the hidden meanings in what he says. The family will merely laugh and be entertained by his performance as he imagines himself to be a valiant Spanish conquistador or a suave French gentleman—all as an excuse to recite in other languages. The language itself transforms him into totally other characters.

After dinner in Chelsea with Aunt Mary and Uncle John, we adjourned to the sitting room, where Edward and Joe were included to join the older men sipping cognac. The ladies retreated to the porch for iced tea. Aunt Mary passed in and out of the room as her children sweetly beckoned her throughout the afternoon to pay attention to their needs until Laura, Aunt Eliza and Aunt Mary succumbed to take a short walk with all the children. It was a beautiful spring day, but I was anxious to slip inside with the men, and indeed was able to accomplish this. I entered as if to look for something, and mocked surprise to find them all there.

Careful not to draw too much attention to myself, I slid onto the sofa next to Uncle John and whispered to him, "May I sit with you a while?"

"Certainly, Lizzie," he responded with a broad smile. I knew he was the one to ask. He caught my father's eye to ensure that no objection would be made and I settled in to listen, and watch, hoping for any excuse to be near Edward.

I thought surely they would excuse themselves into some conversation of political significance, but much to my surprise, they were content to enjoy idle conversation with respect for Joe. No one put a demand on him to speak. I have never seen him as still. He seemed to flip from observing the other men with wonder to watching his own thoughts rambling silently inside his head.

"Edward, how are your studies progressing?" Father asked. Edward took this as an opportunity to capture center stage, allowing me to gaze shamelessly at him.

"I have not been ushered out once since my return to Harvard. I do believe I will pass one more year successfully. Trés bien?" he nodded to my father. "Or should I say, mucho bueno?" I knew that was for me – keeping his promise not to speak French to me.

"So, you are continuing your language studies?" Uncle John laughed.

"Yes, I find them most entertaining, and a nice break from the rigors of studying the law."

"Entertaining?" Father questioned.

"Why, yes. I have come to suspect that my Spanish professor was a matador in his younger years. He has grown old and feeble so makes a dreadful scholar, but he harbors experiences of much more gallant times."

"Tell us more, son!" Uncle John encouraged the story.

"Oh yes. I do," Edward teased. "He teaches—or shall I say 'taunts'—his pupils as if we were nothing more than bulls, daring us to charge forward with our recitations only to mock us for our ignorance. Swoosh! There goes another young and fearless scholar charging into his red cape, or red ink pen, as the case may be."

Joe, laughing and relaxed, allowed Edward's antics to engage him in the gathering. Edward talked not only with his mouth, but his hands contributed wild gestures that drew the listeners to his stories. Father's eyes followed each movement until he too was laughing. That encouraged Edward to continue.

"Each pupil has one or two peccadilloes jutting from his back, as we race around trying to win our teacher's favour. See?" He stands and begins to turn, as if to show off his own.

"That would be a sight to behold. You poor fellow," Uncle John scoffed in mock sympathy.

"Nothing there, of course, I remove them for special family visits." Edward winked at Joe. "I would say that pursuing romance languages at Harvard is the best entertainment I have seen in any theater, but for the fact that I have been scarred once too often in the process."

I expected to hear Father add a sober tone to the afternoon by educating Edward to the seriousness of his studies, but nothing of the sort was ever ushered from his lips.

The afternoon passed quickly. Too soon, Father, Edward and Joe were preparing to return to Somerville. They departed after heartfelt good-byes and numerous kisses, 'tho I was left hoping for something else in addition – a note from Edward. Aunt Eliza, Laura and I remained to enjoy a night's sleep – I wishing Edward's message was under my pillow. Consoled only by the company of my sister and aunt, we rode the morning train back to Salem where I would wait patiently, as well as I could, for my next letter from Edward.

CHAPTER 15

———— ⚬◦⚬ ————

Joe Improves

Joe's physician at Somerville, Dr. Luther Bell, was recognized with the Boyleston Prize from Harvard in 1835 for his essay on diet. His treatment for diseases of the mind likely included 'moral treatment' initially established by the Quakers, occupational activities, recreation, fresh air (ventilation); whereas, physical diseases were generally treated with bloodletting. Joe's assistant physician, Dr. Chauncey Booth, became hospital superintendent in 1856.

———— ⚬◦⚬ ————

Miss M. Lizzie Andrews
Care of Gen. J. Andrews
Salem
Masstts.

Cambridge, [Monday] May 17th 1852

Dear Lizzie -

"Oh! Conscience!" you say when you see this, "What absurdity! I asked him to write the first of the week, and now his letter reaches Salem almost as soon as I myself. I should have thought he could have waited a few days." Perhaps you will think thus when Edward brings my letter from the post-office, but I shall understand your request literally, Cara cugina,[1] (have I spelt it right?) and take the very first opportunity I have of writing to you. I fulfill my promise so early in hopes of receiving a letter from you the sooner, although I always have enough to tell you at any time.

I was unable to give you my note today and I must send it in this without any apology for making my letter so dreadful long. I shall expect a longer letter from you within a week and I shall feel very much disappointed if I have to wait a fortnight. Be sure and destroy the note the moment you have read it.

Joe enjoyed his visit in Chelsea very much and on his way home he appeared as happy as he could be. He said that he was *very* glad to have seen you and he seemed to care more for home than I ever knew him to before. We reached Somerville just before dark and after leaving Joe with a promise to call again soon, I conversed a few moments with Dr. Booth, telling him how much gratified Joe was, how well you all thought him and how much he desired to leave the asylum. What was my surprise when Dr. B- told me that if Joe continued to improve as he had done since he first went out with me, he could probably go home before long. Bravissimo!!! This was so directly opposed to what I had been told that I was as much surprised as delighted. I hope from what Dr. Booth said, that Joe may return to Salem in course of a few weeks; but I would not mention this to him if you write, as he may be disappointed not to go home immediately. I mean to see him this week if I can, and I shall try to have him accompany me to the Dusseldorf gallery on Thursday afternoon, as he is very anxious to see the paintings there. If JW does go to Salem, then I shall certainly pass the first leisure Sabbath I have, with you, (and I want to go very soon) so I will say all I can to favor his return. You see how very selfish I am; but it is natural to almost every one.

Mark the punishment I receive for my selfishness. I am writing this during Prof. Lovering's recitation (for I shall have no other time today) and I had not finished the last sentence before he called upon me to recite. Fortunately I was well prepared and made a brilliant "squirt" (the college word) about "the rarefication and condensation of air," the air-pump &c. I have three exercises after dinner and so I am obliged to improve every opportunity I can find. You mustn't scold me for writing during recitation for your first letter was written in Miss Ward's schoolroom. You see I don't forget your peccadilloes and you must be careful to conceal them. We are obliged to sit a whole hour at every recitation and each usually recites for three minutes once a week in every study, so that I have, at any rate, all but five minutes of an hour to write. I suppose, by this time, you are at home and very sorry, I know, to be there, after five weeks in New York. If *somebody* was only in Salem instead of in New York, you could not help being contented, but now you must feel very "sad and lonely." I wish I could sympathize with you. By "somebody" I mean Cate Pollard of course! (You will allow me to spell Kate with a C. this time I know.) But you must excuse me till after dinner, for it is time to end recitation. "Addio" –

3-P.M. I have only one hour before the Spanish recitation so I can't finish yet, but I will not make another breakage. Don't forget my message to Miss Kate Pollard when you write to New York. If I could see the charm you bought, I would send some message apropos, but now I must trust entirely to your own judgment. If you think it is very pretty, tell her I send my quantity of love and say she is an angel at least. If it is only tolerable, say I thank her very much, hope to meet her soon, am her "trés-humble, trés-obeissant et trés-fideleserviteur[2] and – ahem

- that I should be most happy to render her any service that lies within my power. I wish you would allow me to write a note to your New York correspondent some time, in your name, and then I can say what I choose. I will do so when I come to Salem and you must not object.

Today is too lovely to stay in doors. I wish I had staid in Chelsea all night, had driven you to Salem this morning, or done something equally foolish. I don't know when I shall feel like studying again, for I long to be away from Cambridge for a week or two. This is the reason why father used to oppose my visiting Salem often during term-time, because he said it took away my attention from my studies for a long time afterward. But he is mistaken, as I can study any time I choose.

Our "May recess" commences next Tuesday and continues till Sunday night. I shall pass a day or two of it in Methuen unless I meet father before then. I wish I could go to Salem, but that is impossible and I must not think of it. JW will probably be at home the whole week. He is freed from study after "class-day," and will stay in Salem I suppose, while I, poor Junior must "dig" away till July 21st. But I shall have my turn next year.

I hope you won't think, from my complaints about every-thing, that I am discontented at college. Far from it; I am as pleasantly situated here as I could be anywhere, and I enjoy myself better than I could elsewhere.

Would it not be an excellent idea, if I could train a dog to go between Salem and Cambridge to act as a post-master between us? "It would save postage" and there is something so decidedly romantic about it that I am tempted to make the attempt. You know that I am strangely inclined towards anything romantic, and that I would take a great deal of pains to accomplish the same end differently from other people. Of course you must aid me in training our greyhound postmaster. Imagine him running to Salem some time as fast as he can go with a roll of nonsense about his neck taking as good care of it as if it were treasure.

I always dislike to see the end of my letter so near and particularly tonight. It reminds me of my last visit in Salem, as I sat watching the clock, which seemed to move uncommonly fast, because I wished it to go slower. But I can say no more this time. Be sure to write a *very* long letter to me *very soon*. Good bye.

Ever your aff. Cousin,

E -

1. Cara cugina is Spanish for "dear cousin."
2. French for "very humble, very obedient and very faithful servant."

Enclosed in the letter, folded on a small note, I found these words written in Edward's hand.

> Lizzie,
> You dare not, need not, say a word,
> for your true thoughts I do know.
> I am more alive, less absurd
> when I see your beauty glow.
> My thoughts of love hide by day,
> Illuminate by night,
> In your presence, I do know
> Your eyes see through my soul.
>
> Your Ned

---

22 May 1852

After reading my letter from my dear cousin I pondered whether to give Kate Pollard "a quantity of love" from Edward, or if I might rather thank her and tell her how he hopes to meet her soon as her "very humble, very obedient and very faithful servant." Oh, that he would be as much to me and render me any service that lies within his power. I simply cannot trust what he might say to Kate should he write to her directly—for, once said, his words cannot be unsaid!

Today I am headed to JW's house. I thought he would arrive home from Cambridge in due time for the Sabbath but to my good fortune I hear he has arrived today in time for dinner.

Before I could take my leave this morning, Laura and I were fitted for dresses. The silk is of the most luxurious sky blue I have ever seen. Our dresses will be fashioned differently, of course. Laura's has a small collar of the same yardage that reaches up toward her chin and I have one of a lighter color that folds over along the neckline. It is a most clever style for while it is not at all revealing, there is no stiffness against my neck. The undersleeves on my dress are also of this second color and I have bows that line the entire length of the dress from the collar to the hem. I asked Aunt Eliza what we should do about Joe's shirt, but I do not think it an easy task for Father's tailor to go to Somerville!

As I approached Grandmother Sprague's house I heard someone calling, "Lizzie Andrews is here! Mother, Lizzie is coming to the door!" It is funny to think the family still refers to this home on the corner of Essex and Dean as Grandmother Sprague's house, for she passed on so long ago. Uncle Joseph had lived here with Aunt Sarah for many years until his death three months ago. As I reached up to the door knocker, I saw a small face peer out from behind the draperies covering the side window, next to the door. I recognized little Eddie Smith. The door opened, and Eddie ran away from the door giggling, as I was greeted by Cousin Carrie.

"Good afternoon, Carrie. I am surprised to see you here."

"Lizzie Andrews! I can *imagine* your surprise for I have yet to venture out of this house to bid greetings to anyone. We only arrived last evening from Warren. What a delight to see you." Eddie's little head peered out from behind her dress.

"Hello there, Eddie," I coo'ed. He ducked behind the folds of cloth with a squeal.

"Do come in. What brings the pleasure of your call, Lizzie?"

"Actually, I do not mean to stay. I was calling on JW. I heard he was home from Harvard and I thought he might be so kind as to deliver something to Cousin Edward upon his return." I felt the heat rise to color my face at the mere mention of Edward. The poise I had to muster to refrain from revealing any unusual fondness was trying, indeed.

"I am sure he would be happy to do so. Is it papers he needs for school?"

"No, merely a pocket watch charm."

"I am sure JW can assist and Edward will appreciate your gift."

"Gift? Oh, it is merely a token from my trip to New York – purchased by our host Kate Pollard. In fact, Father and I have just returned from a five-week visit." There. That should lessen any suspicion. "Kate asked if I might deliver it to Edward on her behalf, but I do not know when I might see him next."

"Come sit for a moment Lizzie, while I call JW," which she did by merely raising her voice with the sweetness of a song, before proceeding to loop her arm thorough mine and lead me into the house, all the while continuing to talk, "So, you were five weeks in New York? You must join me for tea and tell me all about your trip." Her invitation to sit could not be politely refused, so I settled in to the parlor chair while she left the room to order tea and ensure her call had reached JW. I must say I had no shortage of things to say, for she welcomed my stories with the utmost graciousness. It was nearly two hours before I was again on my way down Chestnut Street. The blackberry charm was entrusted to JW to transport and personally deliver to my dear cousin.

Walking home I greeted the late afternoon warmth with new respect for the fresh air. The offshore breeze had just rolled in from the harbor and seemed to follow me all the way home.

———— ·∞· ————

5 June 1852

Aunt Augusta had a baby girl yesterday. She has been named Augusta Sprague Tenney. Liz sent word to Aunt Eliza that mother and baby are fine. Aunt Margaret is running the household during Aunt Augusta's lying in, though Aunt Eliza thinks they will need another hand since Senator Tenney is ailing. Oh, how I wish it could be my hand. I could tend to Aunt Augusta while Edward tended to his father, though no one has asked for my assistance, so I must assume they are faring well without me.

CHAPTER 16

Helping Father in the Wide, Wide World

The Wide Wide World, a novel by Susan Warner, published in 1850, was exceedingly popular, selling 20 million copies at that time. Its fictional story of a young orphan gives the reader a picture of life to which people aspired at that time – a life of piousness and faith.

Miss M. Lizzie Andrews
Care of General J. Andrews
Salem
Masstts.

Methuen, [Friday] June 11th 1852

Dear Lizzie -

How! What! Why does he date his letter at Methuen in term time? Is he suspended again? It *is* discouraging, I know, to have a cousin (and that cousin a steady, upright youth from the country) who can't stay two successive years in college without disgracing himself, breaking his neck or falling into some difficulty. I should not dare to ask for pardon from any one else, but I have courage enough to expect forgiveness from "the well-known goodness of your little heart" (don't laugh! I'll tell you from whom I quote, some time) and I *implore* you to forgive me *this once* and consider me as much your cousin as ever, notwithstanding my leaving college. I assure you, a second dismissal has not troubled me much. "It is nothing, when one is used to it." My heart is iron now and I am unmoved by any feelings of remorse or pain. In fact I have become so hardened that I am *determined* to conduct myself no differently when I return, than I have done the last year. Though I have been obliged to leave college I am certain that I shall not pass my time in Warren (alas! Miss Sedgwick!) I shall try to remain in Essex county. Will Miss Ward be my instructress till I return? At what price will you teach me Latin, Italian, Needlework, Embroidery, horse-back riding, knitting, music, &c?

This is all fudge, cousin (I won't say nonsense or you will apply it to the whole letter) and if I thought you believed it I would begin again. It is true that I am now in Methuen, and that I *was* obliged to leave Cambridge, yet that is not the consequence of any wrong-doing of mine. Of course I am perfectly willing to leave college, though under any other circumstances I should feel very sorry to do so.

Father is so ill that he can attend to no business and he was unwilling to have it all neglected so he sent for me to aid him as far as possible. I shall remain at home till he recovers, probably till the beginning of next term. I was called away from college very suddenly and had barely time to see JW on his return from Salem, and tell him why I went away.

Dr. Peirson will call to see father tomorrow or on Monday and I can better form an opinion about his recovery. Now I think there is no doubt but that he will be well soon. My whole time is occupied by him and I have none to myself till everyone else is asleep. Then I am not as free as in Cambridge; for I stay with father every night and have to be with him after eleven o'clock usually.

JW presented me with a fine ripe blackberry at parting, which I have since worn on my watch-chain to the no small wonderment of the Methuen gentry. This gentry pronounce it "real slick" &c but, mirabile dictu, they say "I swow it ain't a real plum." Truly, cousin, I think Miss P's [Kate Pollard's] gift decidedly unique and very pretty. I suppose by her sending me a berry she wished me to bury her image deep in my h-(boots!). You may send her any message from me you choose, provided she isn't "over thirty and unmarried." If she is I shall consider the charm a gift from you. It will be useless for you to say nay, for I have it in my possession and certainly you sent it to me.

I have read the "Wide, Wide World" since I wrote to you in expectation of seeing myself portrayed in full colors, as large as life. I confess I dreaded to meet myself and I trembled like a granite wall when I began the book; not because I am so very formidable but I was afraid that I might be "shown up" to the public gaze, and I should dislike to meet a novel character of which 99 parts were faults and one part good. Still by straining every nerve, I had courage enough to begin the book and looked anxiously for "John." Chapter after chapter was passed yet no "Giovanni" appeared. What an excellent comparison, thought I; I am likened to a nobody; am considered a cypher! That is too bad. "Better be thought a villain than a nonentity"- Still I read on till John entered just as I was leaving the first volume. Of course I welcomed him gladly, but was surprised when I would have shaken hands with a noisy, boisterous fellow, to find such a sober, dignified youth. She has made *one* mistake in the outset, I thought. But I was rejoiced to see that as soon as he entered he kissed every one present. Perhaps that is the cause of my being compared to him. Now don't you ask "Kate" (Miss P_____ I should say) any impertinent questions about that Walk. If you do, *beware the consequences*. Good bye - Au revoir –

Excuse my abrupt termination, cousin cara, (I have another cousin Carrie,) but Father woke up and I had to go down and stay with him the rest of the night. But I must finish about John. The more I saw him the better I liked him, till when I had finished I considered him a paragon. If strangers think I am like the John Humphries in the wide, wide world, I hope none who know me will do anything to change such an opinion. Why *he* never even *thinks* wrong, much less acts wrong. He seems to have almost every desirable quality and is as pure from evil as - as - why as my youngest sister. John is noble-hearted, loved by everyone; he never injures nor speaks ill of any one. One thousandth part of his excellence would satisfy me. I hope you said nothing to change any such opinions in regard to me.

I might retort, and tell you some opinions I have heard others express in relation to a cousin of mine, but I promise you most of them are nearer the truth than that of which you told me.

Do you know why Joe does not write me? I passed my last Sabbath away from home with him and he promised to write to me as soon as he saw his father, who went to Somerville the next day I suppose. I know he would have written me if he had gone home.

Father's sickness will render uncertain perhaps postpone altogether my intended Sunday with you. But if you go to Cambridge on class-day I shall certainly see you. I will go to Salem when I can, but can not promise to stay unless father entirely recovers.

The Osgoods were at Uncle John's when I was last in Boston, but I did not see them. Can't you come home with Emily Oliver some Sabbath? Write me if you do. Mary O. is the wildest girl I ever saw. I met her going to Salem this week.

Thank you, dear cousin, for writing so early and do write me soon again too. Margie frequently asks me about Lizzie Andrews and sends all sorts of messages.

Good bye - Write a long letter - Your Frere -
Edward Tenney

I asked Liz why she didn't write to you. She told me to ask you why you don't write. She says she wrote last to you - Let me have a letter before Class day.

———————————❧———————————

18 June 1852

I wrote in my diary instead of writing a letter so I can speak freely and fear no judgment. I consider that 'mirabile dictum,' though I'd refrain from using the Latin phrase publicly, or even in a letter, to say it is truly 'wonderful to say.'

It used to trouble me to no end when Edward asked me to explain my brother's behavior. "Why does Joe not write?" Should I let my baser self emerge, I would snap, "Ask him yourself for I do not know why my brother does anything he does." Now, I am resigned to the fact that I do not understand Joe's motivations and I am *not* suited to be my brother's keeper. Were his behaviors in any way clear even to himself, I trust they would be clearer to me, as well as all the rest of this wide, wide world. Oh, if life were only as pure and compassionate as that book portrays it to be, we could rest assured that love prevails over tragedy.

Certainly for a young girl like Ellen to lose her mother so young is a tragedy, but that is a common occurrence, and we learn to carry on, though it does put the fear of death in me to think that even I too could meet such a fate when I marry and bear children. How easily are fears such as that overcome when one is filled with the love of another and the strong hand of destiny. If I am to be a wife and mother, it will

203

be. It is not my place to determine if it is to be, and whether it is to be with Edward! However, I do trust and pray that he will make it so. Perhaps we would defy the risks and have a robust family like his mother's childhood family. The Bartletts had fifteen children!

I slapped my diary shut with dismay over my incessant rambling. Oh, conscience, what am I thinking! I have such a considerable amount to learn before I could be fit to head a household half that size.

I fear I am becoming more like the vain ladies who sit like ornaments around the holiday table thinking of gifts, unlike Ellen who restrains herself to the pious life of studying only the most appropriate literature. Oh! Pooh! Could I ever be so self-sacrificing?

Beginning to lift myself from my writing table, I sat down again and questioned myself. Why do I not write Liz? Instead I indulge in descriptions of the glamour of my travels to New York. I sincerely intended to write her from there but for the busyness of my days. Before that I had no excuse save for the demands of my own schooling, and of course, I use my spare Saturdays writing to Edward, rather than his sister. Now, I must delay no longer in writing them both.

I shall tell Edward ever so kindly that he must answer his own question about why my brother does not write him.

Father again went to Somerville to see Joe, but Joe has not yet traveled as far as Salem. He has not been home for such a long time. Father says he is improving, but we do not know when to expect him home and Father thinks it best we wait until his doctors are certain he has recovered, for they say the tendency to fall again into this type of illness is very strong.

I do hope Edward's father improves. The Tenney family is blessed to have such a dutiful son as Edward to take charge of the household during his illness. With due respect for my brother, it would create a disaster if something were to become of Father, and Joe was the only one who could make the arrangements we needed for our well-being!

Oh, absurd! I shant think as much. 'Twil never happen. I could more likely depend on Edward, too. Aunt Augusta and her four children, including her new baby, are not the only ones to rely on Edward to stand in for Senator Tenney. Liz and Mary also have no one else to depend on – only their father and their brother Edward. How blessed am I!

———❧———

25 June 1852

I am to go to Harvard without an escort and know no one there but Edward and JW, both of whom shall likely be consumed with their social duties. Edward has not seen his chums since he left Harvard to attend to his father's business and all must be eager to hear of the causes of his latest departure from the fine establishment of Harvard College. I shall return from there directly to Hamilton but now, I have a weeklong recess from my school. Although I enjoy my studies in Hamilton, I wish at times to be closer to family, perhaps especially since my prolonged stay in New York.

———❧———

I settled in at the Fellows the night before class-day. I was met with much astonishment by my aunt and uncle when they heard I was to attend class-day unescorted. I assured them I would stay with JW, although we all knew he would be most busily involved in the activities of the day. Only I knew Edward would find me, for we had made an oath after class-day last year as to where we would meet. I had no fear that our rendezvous would not be successful. Well, maybe I had a bit of apprehension to be honest, but nothing that would keep me from fulfilling my promise to Edward. I was seventeen years old, for heaven's sake. I was well equipped to venture out alone, even as a lady.

The sun was breaking through the gray sky as I left Chelsea on the train to Cambridge. Edward had arrived at Harvard early on the morning train from Methuen. I saw him across the square, at the exact spot on the large campus where we planned to meet. He had no shortage of company in his presence, and I imagined he had numerous long stories to purport about his exploits as an Esquire in Methuen. The walk across the plaza felt endless. Edward was waiting and my limbs carried me as fast as they could, my heart pounding from anticipation and exertion. I could slow neither the pace of my feet nor the race of my heart. Edward had not yet spotted me, yet I could already see he was engaged in pleasant conversation. Finally, I stepped into the square and caught his eye. He completed bidding his companion good-bye just as I came into reach.

"So good of you to come, m'lady," he beckoned with a slight bow and took my hand planting a sweet kiss upon it. It made me laugh. Did he think we were living in 18th century England? There was no way of stilling the romantic in Edward, and it was not possible for me to be upset with such charm, however exaggerated it may be.

"Good day, Edward. I am so very glad to see that you are already here, for I have felt myself to be something of a spectacle walking alone."

"You are a spectacle, Lizzie. A magnificent one, I must say. You know there is no where else I would be. In fact, I have been here for an hour to be sure nothing stood in my way of greeting you."

"Oh, my!" was all I could muster, considering the circumstances of the public situation. Truly, I wished to reach my arms around his neck and clasp my hands behind him like a necklace. I longed to feel his arms wrap around me and hold me in a passionate embrace, blind to what anyone might say. "Oh, my." I said again as if to still my own imagination. Now he laughed. He must never know the thoughts that run through me.

"Chum, you have returned! With nary a speck of tar nor a feather in sight." The voice came from a strikingly attractive man who approached Edward. He looked to be Edward's age, and even bore a slight resemblance, though he was several inches taller, and towered over me. He placed a firm hand on Edward's shoulder and peered dramatically over it as if to inspect for remnants of tarring and feathering, the telltale signs of disgrace.

"I plucked the last one from my back side just a moment before your arrival. How are you, b'hoy?" Edward bellowed a warm laugh and raised his arm as if to return the pat on the shoulder. He seemed to catch himself in a moment of self-consciousness, opting instead to reach his right hand toward Wilson for a hearty handshake. I knew I was the cause of this sudden gallantry, for Wilson raised an eyebrow as if to notice me for the first time.

"Good day, Miss."

"Oh, excuse me." Edward said. "Miss Andrews. Please forgive me." He looked at me sweetly. "Lizzie, meet my chum, Mister Davies Wilson. Wilson, my cousin, Miss Lizzie Andrews."

"A pleasure to meet you, Mr. Wilson." I was sure I should offer my hand, but standing next to Edward, it suddenly felt too heavy to lift, as if weighted down by the thick heat. Nothing moved easily. Not even the breeze could budge the air. Thankfully, Wilson was already engaging in a slight bow on my behalf and had I raised my hand I might have met his forehead in a most impolite manner.

"The pleasure is certainly mine, Miss Andrews." He quickly turned to Edward, "Your cousin?"

Edward just smiled, and followed Wilson's eyes back to me. They both seemed to notice my dress and I suspected they had never seen one made of such fine silk before. The temperature seemed to rise rapidly in those few moments and I was thankful to have brought a fan. I opened it with too loud a snap and it seemed to startle Edward out of his daydream, or the seemingly close inspection of my new silk dress. Clearing his throat, he looked around and spoke.

"Shall we proceed to the church? I think we are not too early, and it may help us find a seat."

"Oh, yes. Let us." My hand had regained its strength and easily found its way to Edward's elbow.

"Wilson, will you join us?" Edward asked.

"Absolutely. I was headed that way myself."

Our plan to arrive early at the church was successful and we were seated in plain view of everything, but Edward was in and out of his seat, responding to the greetings of his fellow scholars, and inquiries as to his recent whereabouts. After introducing me, I remained seated and silent, yet very pleased to be safely situated between Edward and Mr. Wilson. Wilson also seemed to be examining every bow on my dress. When I caught his eye, he turned immediately away so no conversation was yet attempted.

I looked at my dress to see what might be the distraction and decided to wear my blue silk dress to Commencement.

Wilson interrupted my thoughts, "While Edward is attending to his social obligations, I thought you might enjoy a distraction."

"A distraction?" I whispered.

"Yes," he spoke into my ear, "if you look about you, it becomes quite plain that Harvard College is quite mild and liberal. The reason for this being its purpose to send young gentlemen like me and Edward into the world with all we need to become respectable citizens. Do you think it is working?"

"I would say so," I responded, thinking his comment both strange and apparent and questioning the close proximity of his face to my ear. He continued.

"For scholars like us, class-day is the most important day of our college years. Shame the orator who does not understand it is the best day to get our attention."

I looked up, straining to view the orator, but he had not yet arrived. Last year, my apprehension of being caught in a large crowd had kept me from even attempting to enter the church. Wilson leaned toward me again and tapped his finger in the air to garner my attention to the sights and sounds of the crowd. His smile was warm with teeth quite straight and even, unlike those of so many people. My face flushed with heat as I realized I examined him in a most inappropriate manner. Lizzie, say something! Stop staring, I reprimanded myself as a cruel mother might. Where has my wit fled? Turning from Mr. Wilson, I began to gaze about with mock interest.

His gesture of kindness helped me appreciate the importance of the day, and the interest in the people, many of whom were unfamiliar to me but who so engaged Edward.

At that moment, the orator entered and Edward quickly took his seat. I must admit I was challenged to concentrate on the message, for extreme contentment filled me sitting next to Edward, hearing his calm and steady breathing. Out of the corner of my eye, I could see his fine profile. His nose was perfectly straight emerging from his masculine brow. His chin was strong, his lips looked soft and smooth and I could almost feel the warmth they held, remembering when they touched my own. My heart heard my thoughts and I placed my fan just so, so as to not reveal the throbbing there.

I witnessed more than merely the events of class-day. People in attendance were arrayed in their finest apparel. Never have I seen so handsome a crowd—not at all like I expected when I fled the scene the previous year. But, I was much younger then, it seems, not yet confident to face such an event. Edward exuded a pride befitting a member of such a prestigious society.

My thoughts were interrupted by the orator's proclamation that the scholars had 'indeed prepared well for a life as a respectable citizen.'

———————

Today, having returned safely to Salem from a full week in Hamilton following a most memorable class-day, I am enjoying leisure time. I should like to write Edward but for the fact that I wrote him already from Hamilton—just yesterday! I could not wait a moment longer to send a note thanking him for his hospitality at class-day. I also wish to extend an invitation to join the 4th of July activities in Salem. I do hope the magnificence of the Independence Day celebration is sufficient encouragement for Edward to travel, if he is able. I do so wish I could promenade with my dear cousin in my own town as we did in Chelsea after class-day. Nothing gives me more pleasure. My invitation should arrive in Methuen in time for an abrupt departure. I can almost see it now—Edward dashing off on his thoroughbred stallion racing against the iron horse, his dog galloping in the dust trail just behind, training to make the journey some day on his behalf. Such is the contagious quality of romanticism!

In addition to the invitation, I offered Edward the temptation of horse-back riding while he was here but warned him that I am not fit for such activity, though in truth, I am likely to be as fit for riding a horse as he is for dancing a polka. In due course, I am certain I could tolerate a ride of some duration with him, but such an adventure would not be prudent now for reasons of a female nature that I could ne'er discuss with Edward. I prefer that he suspect my decision is influenced by my previous experience sliding from the saddle, as I did 'once-up-on-a-time' when riding with other ladies. Oh, it was a most distressing display of my equestrian abilities—and the thought of ever doing so in front of Edward! Oh conscience! I could not show my face again. In fact, I have not again ventured to reveal my countenance at the riding school in Ipswich, though I am sure doing so would improve my ability, not to mention my comfort atop one of those tremendous beasts. Any skills I may have gained in my first and only riding school tutelage are surely lost on account of that mishap.

———— ❧ ————

9 July 1852

Edward did not come to Salem for the 4th of July, and I have not received a word from him. His father's illness continues to advance, and Aunt Augusta has a young baby that surely is demanding much of her attention. It has been too long indeed since we were together in Chelsea. I have not seen him since we met at class-day. Has he so soon forgotten how splendid the day was for us both? I will never forget it.

I am to wrap up my studies in two weeks. I long for a nice holi-day with Edward in Methuen before he is to return to Harvard for his final year. Why does he not write? Oh heavens! Is this now the proverbial question that plagues the hearts and minds of estranged family members?

———— ∽ ————

Kate Pollard writes me from New York requesting every detail of Edward's accomplishment. I have taken to informing her using a code we devised when I was in New York. I shan't reveal its secret except to say I tell her where I have gone with the blackberry charm 'she' gave me in New York. It is clear how fond I am of that particular charm, and I can express my enthusiasm for it in a most revealing discourse. In this manner, she will hear what she desires to know, but I avoid any danger of having my feelings for Edward discovered, for as long as we are discreet, there will be no suspicion cast and no interruption of our private outings.

CHAPTER 17

———⁂———

Riding with Margie Phillips

In the mid-1800s, women rarely felt comfortable in public unless they were escorted by men. Wives and mothers—especially middle-class, white women—were seen as guardians of their family's social and moral life. The Industrial Revolution opened new doors for women to expand beyond the private home to engage in reforming society at large through temperance societies, abolitionist organizations and the suffragette movement.

———⁂———

Miss M. E. Andrews
Care of Gen. J. Andrews
Salem
Mass.

Methuen, [Monday] July 19th 1852

Dear Lizzie -

One of the Birds, cousins you know, is very anxious to learn who that lady was with whom I rode home on the evening of class-day. Shall I tell her or send a description of "that lady"? For

I was thinking so much of the enjoyment I had that day, that on my return home I wrote about class-day &c to Hartford and have excited so much curiosity that cousin Martha [Bird] *demands* that her former protégé shall tell her more about his companion to Chelsea and I dare not disobey. I always used to mind her in Hartford and since I left I have refused her nothing. What shall I do? I wish that you were here or that I were in Hamilton. Then you would write to Martha Bird for me & I to Carrie Pollard for you. Now don't say no, because I may ask you some time, and it is possible I may see you before I write again to Hartford. Oh for another class-day!

On the day I left Cambridge (Saturday), Wilson said to me, "Chum that Miss Andrews you introduced me to _____. I can't tell you what W. said but he offered to drive me to Salem whenever I was willing to go (to see the Naumkeag steam mills, I suppose!!). You *must* come to Cambridge next class-day, for my life is greatly endangered by Wilson's threats, if you fail.

Tonight (Monday) I am going to ride horseback with Miss Margie Phillips. She has been taking lessons in Boston all winter and spring and comes to Methuen for eight (or 12) weeks vacation with such a passion for the sport that she is determined to ride as often as she can. The only difficulty is that there is a great scarcity of gentlemen (and Margie P. is dreadfully bashful) so that she must either ride alone (impossible) or take the best she can find. I volunteered to accompany her and (for want of a better, in fact any other, offer) was accepted. She would ride three or four hours, six times a week, but her father (strange to say!) objects to that, so we have to content ourselves with two long rides a week. If I thought you would believe me, I would tell long stories about the martyrdom I suffer &c., but the fact is, that I have a fine time, enjoy myself much and wish we rode oftener.

Gossips open wide their curious eyes, and think *something* must be in course of accomplishment, when the Parson's

214

daughter and the Squire's son so often ride off alone and come back so late; but Margie says *she* don't care and of course *I* have no reason for being disturbed. Oh Lizzie you *must* learn to ride. If in no other way, go to Boston in the cars and attend riding school, the best way to ride well. You see how emphatically I say "must," so you must expect something dreadful if you neglect. Liz and Mary are learning. Liz is preparing a riding habit and will join Margie Phillips and myself as soon as she has courage to appear in the village, in a week, I hope. After a few trials, you will be able to take "Bobby" and with JW make a good long trip; you will be sure to enjoy yourself I know.

10-P.M- Here I had to pause to attend father's call and I have since found no time to continue. Still my labor has been either profitable or agreeable so that I have no reason to regret my breathing-time. After doing what father wished I found one of his clients below and as "the counselor" does not attend to business, his client had to consult the *junior partner:* consequently I had the pleasure of transferring a sum of money from the client's pocket to the purse of the "junior partner."

Since I came home I have been growing quite wealthy from office fees and if I remain a few months longer, I *may* have a fortune to retire upon. When I had completed my business I rode to Andover with father and now I have just returned from my horse back ride. At first we had a dreadful time. The stable horse that Margie Phillips was to ride was unmanageable and it was impossible to obtain another that was suitable. At last after waiting some time for another horse, I changed horses with Margie, she taking mine which she liked very well and I bestrode the unruly steed. This was about seven o'clock and we returned before nine not being able to ride as far as usual on account of the lateness of the hour. (There is no moon now, and it is quite dark by nine o'clock).

215

I received your last letter on July 5th, too late of course to come to Salem for the day; but I thank you very much for your kind invitation, though I should have come without it if I could, relying on the strength of your general invitation. Here is a quotation from one of your letters to me, "I think, dear cousin, that you deserve a severe scolding for writing to me when you should be attending to your studies," i.e. in recitation - Now were I to follow your suggestion, I should say something dreadfully severe (a few days ago, Grace Carleton reminded me that I can, even to you); for your last letter was written in school, and your first one also; perhaps I *might* scold fiercely if you were present, but I promised to find no fault with your letters except on the ground of brevity and scarcity, so that you can have the scolding in anticipation.

I expect to go to Cambridge tomorrow evening for Commencement and I may see you there as JW has probably invited you. I was very glad to hear that he has "a part" and he seems very much rejoiced. If you go to Cambridge on Wednesday I hope you will have better luck in finding some friends than you did on class day and not be obliged to tramp alone about Boston and Cambridge, for you would not enjoy yourself afterwards sufficient to compensate for it. Were not you very tired the Saturday after class-day! I called at the Atlas office before leaving Boston but you had not returned from Chelsea - Write *very* soon, cara cugina.

Addio -
E

Excuse my return to the old habit of effeminate writing, but my paper is so small that otherwise I could not say half enough. Do come to Methuen when you can. Father is not improving now, so that I can not expect to leave home at present. Liz has left school, as she says, for ever and aye –

The Howard Athenaeum opens Sept. 6th for the season and Mad. Thillon is one of the first Stars engaged. You *must* go then and I hope to be in Boston at that time. All would send love, "the youngest" too, if they knew I were writing. Don't fail to ride horseback if you possibly can. "Aunt Lizzie" Felt was here a few days ago for one day - I shall write to Joe soon.

Ladies Rode Side Saddle With Gentleman Escort

26 July 1852

I barely saw Edward at Commencement. I was taken up entirely in the excitement exhibited by Father as JW graduated. I think he carried the spirit of JW's late father Joseph for never before had I witnessed a more demonstrative manner from my father. When I did see Edward it was only with time to exchange a courteous greeting. I was certain to give him a severe scolding for not writing to me after class-day, but could only exchange cousinly promises that we should write more often. I was able to tell him I missed his letters, and he quietly insisted he had just written, not knowing if he would see me at the Commencement. Now, his word is good, for I arrived home to find a nice long letter. In a mere moment, a sheet of writing can make me forget all time and distance that has separated Edward from me. Thank God I have heard today, and he is well and his father must be faring aptly for little mention was made of his health.

I am now more anxious than ever to take a trip to Methuen for a visit, if I would be welcome this summer, as I have been every other year. This summer is unlike any other, however; so I will write both Edward and Aunt Augusta and offer to assist her. Surely she would appreciate help in contending with the demands of the children now that Uncle John needs more of her time. As Edward has assumed his father's business, I wonder if he also sits in his father's place at the head of the table.

At Harvard, Father introduced me to a friend of JW's and proceeded to invite him to join us for tea after the Commencement exercise. Well, as you can imagine, this was not at all to my liking, for the entire family was engaged in conversations, leaving me to entertain "young Mr. Theodore A____." I shan't even say his whole name for I do not want to mock the man, but it was a dreadfully boring time for me, and became more so as the evening progressed and he began to talk about the dancing that was to take place in the evening after supper. I could not imagine wanting to dance with him and deeply regretted, even resented, it was not Edward with whom I was presented the opportunity I desired. Theo. is not to blame. I am sure he is a perfectly fine sort, but he is not Edward. Yet, I did not want to cause any feelings of ill-will on this otherwise celebratory day, and was very plain about my father's reluctance to have me out dancing that evening. That ended up fine, but for the fact that it is a bold-faced lie. I lied in Father's presence but at such low tones that he could not hear. Thank you, God, for not revealing my wickedness at that very moment in front of Father and JW, and poor innocent Theo.

CHAPTER 18

Greatest Imaginable Hurry

Miss M. E. Andrews
Care of Gen. J. Andrews
Salem
Mass.

Methuen, [Thursday] 19th August 1852

Dear Lizzie -

It *is* perfectly convenient; by all means come as soon as you can. I have just received your letter and can write but a few lines before the mail leaves; so I shan't trouble you very much this time.

If you *can* come on Monday or Tuesday or the first of the week, do, and be prepared to stay a long while not "a few days" -

Bring up your riding-habit, and you can at least make a beginning.

Mary & Liz have their habits nearly finished and will ride soon.

You *must* bring the "Merry Zuigara" sheet music too. I heard Joe whistle the first part of it, so I know you can sing it.

Lottie - we call her Jimmie now - has been sick but today is almost as well as ever.

Father went to Weathersfield yesterday, and will return some time next week.

I felt "real bad" not to go back to Hamilton with Joe.

Two days ago, had it rained I should have called and dined with you, but unfortunately it was pleasant, and I remained at home. I was disappointed, but the news of your coming has removed all that.

I shall be waiting for you in the noon train on Monday at Lawrence, and perhaps on Tuesday if you fail to come on Monday.

I have lots to tell you about Cambridge &c.

My poor blackberry needs your assistance.

Don't forget the Zuigara, habit, &c.

Good bye -
Edward

Excuse this lawyer's (?) style & hand, but I am in the "greatest imaginable hurry."

The train pulled up to the station in Methuen Tuesday and I could see Edward standing on the platform. Perhaps due to my not having appeared the day before, he looked more serious than ever I have seen him, until the moment he saw me. In that instant a broad smile spread across his face. I was as excited as a child with new skates on a white Christmas morning and could not keep my own joy suppressed, though I would rather have preferred not every person on the train had seen what came over me.

Edward took care not to run to the door of my car and attract attention, but I have never seen him walk so quickly!

"Lizzie! Dear cousin!" He called as he hurried past my window toward the door. The train was not yet at a complete standstill when he hopped onto the step. There was only one gentleman in front of me queued up to disembark, and when he spotted me as the object of Edward's attention, he stepped back to let me pass. I had only one small carpetbag, which my cousin seized and tossed onto the depot platform like a sack of mail. He reached carefully toward me to help me down.

"Lizzie. Lizzie. Lizzie." He let his arms slip around my waist and swung me completely around before setting me down. The eyes of the kind gentleman burned into me as my petticoats whisked the breeze in his direction. Oh, my.

Edward's vocal enthusiasm was most embarrassing and his behavior... was shocking! I scolded him outright, for all to see. "Edward! Now, Edward! Not so loud. Everyone is looking!"

"Let them enjoy a good long look." He laughed and gathered my bag. I reached for his arm and squeezed it tight as we hurried to the carriage. I cherished his gentle assistance into the carriage and felt so happy to be in Methuen I could not continue my feigned reprimand at his boisterous greeting.

Though it was the top of summer, he brought a coverlet for my lap to assure my comfort as we traveled back to his house. A welcome turn in the bend slid me close to him on the carriage bench, and I did not shift away.

"Lizzie, I am desperately in need of your pleasant company. I have never been so occupied with caring for another. Mind you, I am not suggesting that Father's company is not of the highest order. It is, indeed, but he is sadly approaching the end of his life, whereas I, well, I have much life to live. I fear with his departure I will be ending the carefree beginning of mine. Never have Father and I been at such apparently divers positions – he has never really *needed* me before."

"He is beginning the end, and you are ending the beginning." I

223

repeated his thought, softly absorbed in their meaning. Edward leaned toward me and responded.

"I beg your pardon?"

"Your father. He is nearing his end?" I moved the conversation deeper.

Edward spoke slowly and thoughtfully. "He seemed to be quite fine when he went to Vermont, but upon his return he spoke so joyfully of his trip I was nearly overcome by emotion. Lizzie, it was as if he had voyaged to bid his last 'good-bye'—as if he knew something about what was to come. He gained strength to attend to that necessary task, but weakened rapidly at its completion." Edward fell silent with an expression that showed his thinking continued long after his words had stopped.

"I am so sorry, Edward."

"Oh, Lizzie. Enough of this talk. I am not a bit sorry for a single thing at this very moment and I wish for you to also be free of sorrow. I am so very happy to see you again. Thank you for coming. The entire household is eager for your visit."

"I, too, am happier than you could ever know, merely to spend time near you."

Edward sighed, a long, relaxed breath. I leaned into him and nearly rested my head on his shoulder. I knew that too soon we would be in sight of his father's house and I wanted to bask in his warmth for as long as I could before being called to attend to the affections of the rest of his family.

How could Edward possibly take leave of his attention to his father and return to Harvard for his senior year? His devotion was admirable. He was right to feel he was completing the beginning of his life—one that, I prayed, would be long and rewarding, as his father's has been... one that, I hoped, we would spend together.

Well, the visit did not allow time for us to be alone in each other's company, although it was pleasant enough to hear his voice and pass him as we went about our daily business.

Edward stayed with his father most of the day, reading correspondence and discussing his business affairs. In the evenings, Edward invited me to sit while he read, if the subject was thought to be appropriate and of sufficient interest to a young lady. I found it all of interest, every single thing Edward read, but, of course, I did not dare try to assert this view to his father, or anyone else in the household.

During the day, Aunt Augusta was in constant motion between her husband, her children and the servants. With three young ones and a baby, the household buzzed with activity. Aunt Margaret attended to the new arrival, while Liz, Mary and I entertained Johnny, Maggie and Lottie, who was indeed being called Jimmie, a name that is hard for me to accept for such a darling little girl. We went for a short horse-back ride one afternoon, played music and often sang in the evening, though my greatest pleasure was my time tending to little Augusta. While holding her, I made a point to walk past Edward's father's room. Once, I saw Edward nearly fall out of his chair leaning back to see me in the hallway.

"Lizzie, what have you there?" Edward asked, which I welcomed as an invitation to stop in the open doorway to his father's room.

"I am tending to your baby sister for a few minutes while Aunt Augusta is occupied."

"She looks like you, Lizzie. Come in." He motioned to me. "Look, Father, do you not think the baby bears a striking resemblance to Lizzie?"

"Perhaps a bit. She has two eyes, a nose and a mouth." It was nice to hear Uncle John's humor. "Actually, I think it is Maggie who is growing to look more like her Aunt Lizzie every day."

"I do too, Father. I told Lizzie as much," he said, and turned to me, "Did I not say as much, Lizzie?"

"You did, indeed, but you said you would not flatter me so, if you recall, and I think you have just now broken your word, Edward." His father laughed.

"Lizzie, the boy is inventive with his flattery. One must keep a mindful eye on him." Suddenly more serious, he continued, "Perhaps you will do so, Lizzie, on my behalf, when the day comes that I cannot." Edward turned away from him with such a look of sadness that I did not know how to respond, but Uncle John persisted. "Will you do that, Lizzie?"

"Of course, if you wish. Why, certainly. I suppose." Nothing I said sounded like the right thing to say. "I must bring the baby back, so please excuse me if I leave you two. Thank you for letting us intrude upon your conversation." I was nearly overcome with emotion, for there, at that single moment, I stood in the exact middle of life, looking down into the eyes of a babe in my arms, looking up to a venerable gentleman in what appeared to be his last days, and looking forward to the man of my future dreams.

———⟨∞⟩———

It seemed that in a heavy heartbeat it was Tuesday already. My vacation was coming to a close, and Edward was preparing the carriage to take me to catch a car to Salem. We did not have time for private conversations during my stay, but that was no problem for me. I did not feel I had anything in particular I needed to say.

Edward's father was feeling better that day and went for a walk in the country with a friend who came calling in the early morning. Edward and I left the house nearly as soon as Uncle John had gone and we were an hour early for the train. We drove to the edge of Methuen. We were not far from his home when Edward pulled the carriage to the side of the road by a huge oak tree.

"Shall we stop for a bit, Lizzie?"

"It is a beautiful morning for a stroll. I would enjoy that. Yes." I responded, as if the weather had any part to play in my desire to walk with Edward.

He set the brake and jumped out, cooing soothingly to the horse as he passed in front of him, patting his soft muzzle. He reached up to help me out. There was not much in Methuen to see — scattered farmhouses and seemingly endless rutted roads that today offered the perfect invitation to walk.

"Lizzie, I fear you did not have a relaxing visit, for I could see you were occupied with matters of the household throughout your entire stay."

"I enjoyed being busy. If I could not sit in your company all of the time, I much preferred to have my time well-occupied."

"I would have enjoyed reading together, something of our own choosing, like we did in Salem when you were not well. But of course, I do not wish you to be ill, for heaven's sake."

"I should hope not!"

"Perhaps on your next visit, I will take you for a ride in the carriage to Boston to hear Madam Thillon, or Sontag and Alboni. There are so many things I would like to share with you, Lizzie. I think of you at every concert I attend, imagining you sitting by my side, and then resting your head upon my shoulder as we ride home in the carriage after a full evening of entertainment."

"Edward, you are such a romantic. Do you not listen to the music, or merely fill your head with your own sentimentality?"

"I use one ear for the music, and the other for my silly thoughts of my cousin. See, this ear? It is yours. It is the one you may box when I become utterly absurd and you can no longer bear my boorish, sentimental company."

"That day will never come."

"Well, for that, I am glad. I am elated. I rejoice!" Edward's voice grew louder. "For that, I celebrate!" He spun around and planted himself directly in my path. I nearly walked into him, and before I could step back, he had me completely entrapped in his arms. They wrapped entirely around me and held me. He stopped talking and I stood still. I never wanted to move again. Oh, to be embraced with such firmness and gentleness. He leaned his head forward over my shoulder, nearly resting his chin on me, and then slowly pulled it back, though his grip did not lessen. He looked in my eyes and I dropped my gaze.

I could see my skirt flaring out behind me as he pressed himself into the front of it. The hem must have been nearly off the ground in the back, but there was no one nearby to see a thing of it. We were alone with nature.

"Look at me, Lizzie. I want to look deeply into your eyes."

I raised my head. He released one arm from around me and put his hand between us, touching my chin, I suppose to make sure I did not look away again. Then he moved his mouth slowly toward me and touched his lips to mine. I did not fear that we would be seen, though any one traveling that road would have had a full view. I did not care.

He kissed me for a long time. I wrapped my arms around his waist and let my fingers feel the warmth of his back, and the curve of his waistcoat. His kiss went completely through me. I thought my limbs would fail me and I would drop into a puddle on the road, but he held on so firmly that I knew there was no safer place on earth, no where else that I would rather be. When he pulled his face from mine, he looked directly into my eyes again.

"I will not apologize for that, Lizzie. I have wanted to kiss you like that for so long. I could not bear to let you go away for one more day without a real kiss."

I wish I had found a word at that moment to tell him how I felt. There were no words, only feelings that I could not describe, for they were as foreign to me as anything I had ever known. I will forever remember the exact day and moment that kiss was pressed upon my lips, for it was the most tender attention I have ever received from any-one at any time in my life.

I was too soon on the car and before I knew it the train was pulling into the station in Salem. My mind drifted constantly back to that fleeting morning in Methuen.

4 September 1852

I have been home three days since my visit to the Tenney's and have caused nothing but trouble. Edward's father once told him he thought long visits to Salem distracted Edward from his studies. My own father has somehow adopted this belief, but not for Edward, for myself! Oh, dread.

On Wednesday, I dropped a teacup that once belonged to my mother. It shattered horribly into a million tiny pieces. I cried for the loss as if I was losing my mother all over again. Yesterday, I burned a cake—something I have never done before! Father told me he thinks I am pre-occupied. He chided me to attend more to my daily tasks and studies and less to my dreams or worries about others. He says 'too soon' I will be expected to have gained skills he feels are 'necessary.' Soon? What? Oh, dear me.

I am ashamed at whatever may have come over me to become so careless. Admittedly, my attention was elsewhere. I was reading and failed to watch the oven. Yes, I was reading Edward's last letter and thinking of when I might see him next. In truth, I was thinking of a kiss. Shocking! The kiss Edward gave me when I was in Methuen. I cannot say a word about it, but it is a feeling I want to have every day of my life – a feeling of knowing that everything is meant to be exactly as it is in the moment.

Oh, yes, I know there is ever so much talk among the most eloquent circles of society as to a thing they call 'free will.' Father's reprimand included those dreaded words. 'Lizzie, these mishaps do not happen in and of themselves. You must take control of your own free will if you are to prevent such occurrences.'

But Father must not understand what I feel is beyond anything I could have decided to do or feel of my own free will! I do not want to control my feelings of deep content. I want to surrender to them and to what I hope is indeed my life's purpose. Father says we each have a purpose to make the world a better place for those who live now and those yet to be born. I will someday be a wife. I will someday be a mother. I will someday take my place in society. Sooner or later.

Calmness surrounds me at the thought and penetrates through me like an ocean fog that settles in for a long winter. I am calm to the core, for I have felt true love.

TheEnd
(or the beginning of a beautiful courtship)

Continue reading to enjoy a preview of...

The Courtship of Lizzie Andrews: Will You Marry Me?

<hr/>

Edward has left his father's bedside and returned to Harvard for his senior year and his life is shifting direction.

Chapter 1
Senior Year at Harvard

'Bully for him!' That is what Joe said when I told him the news. Delighted to depart my brother's cruel manner, I have eagerly commenced my daily train ride to Hamilton, for another semester. As I was leaving for the train, Father slipped this letter into my hand.

Miss M. E. Andrews
Care of Gen. Andrews
Salem
Mass.

Cambridge, [Tuesday] Sept. 14th 1852

Dear Cousin -

Oh! College life is charming! Here is one of its oft occurring, pet delights, which always seem to happen so very a'propos. I had my letter but half dated when out goes my lamp and I have to spend half an hour before I can begin again. (I wish my "Goody" was an engineer). But this is nothing.

I shall expect a score of classmates to bore me before I am done.

For the first time since I entered college (a long time ago!) I have this year a decent looking room on the first floor, furnished quite prettily and *very* comfortably. My chum Davies Wilson has a piano and any quantity of music. When you come to Boston this fall, I shall insist upon your seeing the room. Of course I can't help studying very hard now. To be sure, thus far I have been too busy to study much; for in addition to the usual duties of the first of the term, no sooner had I joined my class than I was requested to write and deliver an oration before a society to which I belong. As this is an honor, I could not refuse; so I worked hard till last Friday night.

You can't possibly guess what my studies for this year are. Besides the regular studies I have chosen, as extra, Italian and Hebrew. The Prof. thinks I am going to be a Unitarian minister. In fact my success in this language is tending to make me change from the law to preaching. Would you? At any rate I am going to be pedagogue this winter, provided I can obtain a school. Wilson, too, will try once more to teach, but he usually trains so much among the *young ladies* of his school, that he does not teach much.

When you come to Boston, I have any quantity of Concert tickets for you. Germanian, Musical Fund Rehearsal and concert, Serenade Band &c. I am going to the Ser. Band concert tomorrow afternoon with three or four classmates. Can't you possibly be there? August Fries has returned from Europe and will direct the M. Fund. I am sorry for it, because we shall lose his fine music at rehearsals and concerts for the sake of a directing which some one else might do as well as he. Mlle Lehman is to come soon and will sing all winter for the Quintette club. Madame Thillon will not be in Boston before October, if then even. Sontag and Alboni will be here after the music hall is completed. You must be prepared to stay a long while in Boston when you come and come you will, 'of course.'

15th

I intended to have written you earlier, but have been so very busy, and I knew that you were in no hurry, that I have postponed it from day to day without thinking how fast fled time. On that Tuesday I reached the cars just in time and arrived at home a few moments before father. The next day I decided to go back to college and I left home the Wednesday following, without another farewell ride with Margie Phillips or even seeing her before my departure. That was not my fault however, for she was at Lowell Island. Liz writes me that Margie & herself have rode alone since I left. Have you forgotten to make some arrangement about attending riding school? I wish that you could come to Boston once a week for that purpose. Only think! If you *do*, you can ride from Boston to Salem with Theo. A.!!! You can't resist that temptation I know.

One poor freshman from Salem was treated dreadfully by the Sophomores last right. He is Devereux, so Oliver says. It was raining and about midnight the Sophs carried him from his room and tied him so firmly to a tree in the yard that he remained out doors a long time before he could extricate himself. This might have killed him, and it far exceeds any college barbarity I ever heard of. I have not heard of Geo. Holyoke's being troubled at all yet.

I wrote to Joe some time ago, but I fear he will not like the tone of my letter. I wrote what your father asked me to and I told J. that he must do something soon if he would keep away from Somerville.

Don't think I am falling off in the length of my letters; for this is only once.

Do write as soon as you can and a *very long* letter. Say when you will be in Boston.

Good bye, Cura cuzina -
Ever yours
Edward

Remember! You must come to Boston before Thanksgiving. I am expecting Carrie Wilson at my room with her brother every moment, and he says she will exercise his piano for the next two hours. Excuse my writing but I have scratched this last page in great haste, for fear of Miss W's coming.

www.ingramcontent.com/pod-product-compliance
Lightning Source LLC
Chambersburg PA
CBHW071306250626
47159CB00004B/1330